THE
ESPLANADE

ROBERTA DEWA

Weathervane Press

Weathervane Press

Published in 2014 by Weathervane Press

www.weathervanepress.co.uk

ISBN 978 0 9562193 8 1

Cover painting by Kit Wade who hereby asserts her right to be identified as the artist.
www.kit-wade.co.uk

Printed by Lightning Source

He is lying on his back on the pebbles where the tide has left him, looking up at the sky. A bleached sky, pale as the hair capping his scalp. Not a mark on him, nothing to mark him out as a corpse except for the stillness of the body, the dead white of his eyes. The tide shrinks slowly away, growling over the last of the pebbles, retreating to the sand. He has the beach to himself, except for the gulls and a single figure coming slowly towards him. The figure is a young man, barefoot, jeans rolled up below his knees, a guitar slung behind him. He is singing, his voice clear and tuneful and a little quavery, the chorus of *Love Grows Where my Rosemary Goes*. Over the jeans he has a white open necked shirt and a brown leather jacket, and a woman's hat: a turban confection of white, a train of net blowing out behind him like wings. The singer reaches the body, and stands over it for a moment. Then he bends and feels in the pockets of the sodden jacket. Inside, there is a key, still bright. He holds it up, turns it to catch the sunrise, then pockets it.

A moment to balance the hat securely on his head and he is off towards the town, still singing. Louder, if anything, this time.

The tide turns, and turns again. The seasons scud their light and shadow across the bay. The beach is empty, except for the gulls and a tramp quartering the strandline for flotsam, pocketing shells and bits of coloured glass in his scuffed jacket, flopping down on the pebbles to examine his treasures. In front of him the seaside town stands to attention behind its promenade, hotels fresh painted for the season, the obelisk at the road-end gold-pinning the pallid sky. To the left of the obelisk, a smart hotel with a turret room leaning out from the building like a fresh-caulked ship about to launch; to the right, facing the hotel across the road-end, a dusty pub caged in scaffolding, a sign announcing its refurbishment hanging high up in the steel.

The tramp tips his old Fedora further up his head. Then he fishes deep in his leather pocket, and pulls out an old tobacco tin; blows the tissue lining aside and brings out a key. He holds it up, catching the sunset; he squints at the sign, at the pub, and the smart hotel; then he looks back at the key.

Megan, he says, in a hoarse croak of a voice. Then, *Lynn*. He passes the key from one hand to the other, saying the names again, as if he was playing a game. A game with a question in it.

Whose key? Megan's, or Lynn's?

PART I

1

MEGAN

Wherever I look, things seem to be disappearing. Red phone boxes, railway stations, lighthouses. Corner newsagents with buckets and spades hanging out for sale. Wooden beach huts painted in pastel colours with little kitchens inside them. Old things, things I've got used to, that aren't there any more. They're all vanishing, one by one, not exactly without warning but quietly, completely, without a fight. Gardens are being paved over, old pubs demolished, and the ruins tidied away until there's nothing left to recognize, least of all a name. As Alex says at least once a week, pubs don't have names nowadays, or rather they have the names of the people who own them, always two names, like a firm of lawyers. The old names vanish, their painted signboards taken away in the skip. And the pavement's swept clean of them.

So far the King's Head is hanging on. It still has its own name, still has plush seats and an old red carpet on the floor and a signboard outside with *The King's Head* in scrolling letters and a painting of the king underneath it, the king in profile, like a playing card, his hand held up with the finger pointing and a gold crown on his head. The sign creaks on windy nights; I can hear it when I'm lying in bed. From eleven o'clock in the morning till chucking out time the pub is full to overflowing with people who've been cleared out of the new pubs along with the rubbish, who want to smoke and drink and sit where they like, who put two fingers up to

Diners Only and mottoes on fake beams and paninis. At the King's Head there are no meals, even at lunchtimes, or extractors for the smoke; but there's a jukebox, a real jukebox where you pay a pound for your own five memories and even though you may have to sit all night waiting for them they'll come round in the end, Imagine and Summer the First Time and Misty and The Long and Winding Road and the last one from Dusty, the only woman, doing Goin' Back. That's the order, and though the machine may mix them up I know, I sort them out. When Olive, who's Suspicious Minds and 24 Hours from Tulsa, asked me what I thought happiness was, I said it was your turn on the jukebox. Your own three numbers lighting up on the machine, the words you know and sing along to without anyone hearing you. A feeling like a pin stuck in you from years ago. That's happiness.

And Philip, of course.

It's a Tuesday, so I'm down in the bar early. I find my green plush seat in the corner and smooth away the prints left by other bodies and put my tapestry bag down to show I'm here. I have a big glass of Chardonnay so I won't need to go to the bar very often, because although I'm a resident and they ought to serve me first, they never do. Usually Irish Jerry, who's Turn It On Again and Stairway to Heaven, shouts across at fat Avril for me, waving his free stiff arm with its long brown finger extended like a rifle-barrel. And he'll talk to me while I'm waiting, he knows about Philip and Quetzal and Tuesdays.

'Been to see her today, Megan?'

When Jerry says this he's just being kind. He doesn't really want the details but I say them anyway, and he nods and drinks his Guinness. Today it would have been her birthday so I tell him how excited she would have been, I tell him about the presents. I tell him about the square lavender soap in cellophane, the necklace with red stones and the hanky with yellow flowers. I wanted her initial embroidered in the middle, but you can't get Q so the hanky has O on it, and we just have to imagine the rest. And I took her my perfume bottles. The best one has a sculpture of birds on the top in cloudy glass, beautiful and solemn, just like her gravestone with the lady leaning over it. I tell Jerry you wouldn't look twice at the stone if the lady wasn't there with her hands hanging down across In Memory. I'm never sure if she's an angel or not, although she doesn't have wings. She has a veil over her head, like a wedding veil held in place with a ring of flowers. Poppies, they look like, even though they're white. And she has white eyes behind the folds of the veil, soft and gentle eyes that make me think of something old and folded and kept in a drawer, something I'll never wear again.

And I want to talk about the church and the people coming out of it, but I don't get that far because Genesis are on and Jerry's drumming on the bar and there are slops of Guinness everywhere and by the time he comes back to me it's gone.

'So is he coming to take you away tonight, Megan?'

Maybe, I say. Maybe.

But by now it's eight o'clock. Time to sit down.

I have a routine while I'm waiting. It's about the past, mine and Philip's, the past that makes me remember why he's still with me, the past that spreads into the future like wine round the stem of my wine-glass. I begin by moving the glasses and beer-mats on the table out of the way and wiping the spillages up with a tissue, sweeping the copper until there's just a soft white smear, dotted with tiny circles of exploded bubbles, air that rises into the smoke on the ceiling. Then I take my photographs out of my bag and spread them carefully over the surface of the table. Some of them are ones I took myself, fresh and glossy and white on the reverse; some of them are cut out of old newspapers or college magazines, all of Philip with different dates and names of plays scribbled on them. One play more than any other, the one about the future, *The Shape of Things to Come*.

I read the words on the back of the photo, and then I turn it over, hide the words beneath his face. His beautiful face with its dark and lightness, its blue and white and black, the eyes looking at me, seeing inside my bones and knowing where the holes are, until I can't stand it any more; and I put the photo back till it's a blur again. Then I pick another, and another. When I've been through them all I just wait, freezing myself into stillness and imagining I can dissolve like they used to do in science fiction and rediscover myself in one of the photos with him, curling my hand under his for the pose, waiting for it to be over; and I stay that way for half an hour, while the pub door opens and closes each time with a squeak of pain straight out of a Jacques Tati movie, and the customers come and go.

It's half past nine when he finally comes. As soon as he's through the door and on his way Irish Jerry spins round as if he was on a piano-stool and juts his dirty thumb at me; and then I see him, dressed in his black leather jacket and T-shirt and jeans, walking through the bar and heading straight for me, not greeting or looking at anyone else; and I know it's a bad day, because his eyes are washed-out and looking over my head, looking at something in the distance that I can't see. I grab my photos and sweep them back inside my bag and knock my glass off the table and without a word Philip turns on his heel and calls to Ralph to get me another Chardonnay.

He brings the drinks and slams my glass down without a beer mat. The wine runs down the stem, pools round the bottom of the glass.

'Shit day,' he says. 'Just total shit.'

I'm very quiet when he says this. I keep still and wait while he drinks his bourbon, I wait for him to remember what day it is, to say her name. Quetzal, I say, Quetzal, down to the floor, trying to pass it on to him, trying until it fades into the music. Diana Ross is on, with Ain't No Mountain High Enough, then A Hard Day's Night, and then Misty three times in succession with nothing in between. I know that's Alex, but I leave it to Jerry to shout at him, I'm keeping quiet, just miming to Diana and the others.

Then I make a mistake. I move my hand to get a beer mat and Philip sees one of the photos I didn't get back inside my bag in time and he grabs it and tears it into pieces and throws them on the floor.

'I'm here, aren't I? So you don't need this shit.'

I look at the floor. The bits of photograph are floating in the wine and curling up at the edges. It's one of the college ones, from the old days when we first met. The paper is thin, soaking the wine up like seaweed, turning back into pulp. Underneath the table I'm holding my bag against my stomach like a cushion, like the hot water bottle I used to hold there for my stomach ache.

Philip's head is down over his drink, his white fringe screening his forehead so I can't see his face. The table is empty, blank, wiped clean. Tonight, it's better that way, I understand.

When Ralph has called last orders a couple of times Philip pushes his glass away and gets my hand and pulls me to my feet, takes me through the door at the back of the bar marked Private and up the stairs. The carpet treads are sticky, they suck your steps out of you if you go up too

11

slowly; they glue you to the wood underneath like an Elastoplast that's been on too long. The carpet peters out on the landing and there's the sound of someone coughing, or retching, behind the first of the numbered doors on the right. At the fourth door we stop and I take my Yale from my pocket and turn it in the lock, push the door and stand back to let Philip go in first.

Inside, the room is green: the bed, the bedside table, the fridge, the washbasin, all bathed in the green light that gives the room its atmosphere, coming from the lamp with the green shade and black fringe I found on the market and put on the bedside table. Since I got it I hardly use the top bulb any more. The light drapes the room like an old dress that smells of joss-sticks, it makes the furniture soft, like those watches Salvador Dali painted; it melts the hard edges from everything. Philip moves into the spotlight cast by the lamp until it's only a jump from where he's standing to the quilt, taking off his jacket and chucking his keys at me the way he always does, waiting for me to catch them before he moves again. Then he's falling with me, into the green billows of the quilt like it was a parachute dropped round us, and with the jump over all we have to do is lie there safe and cushioned and feel the soft ground underneath us.

Afterwards, when the colour comes back to his eyes, he'll remember.

And then I dream. They're vivid dreams, the kind I always have. Only I don't dream of Quetzal, I dream of being in the bar, and the jukebox stalling again. The records are stuttering around their circle like they always do, standing up on their edges like black plates in a rack, waiting for their turn to play; and then, when it's time for my last selection the disc comes out of its slot but doesn't flip over and drop down onto the turntable. It just hangs there, on the end of the plastic arm, with the arm sticking out as if it was paralyzed. And I can see the dark blue of the Decca label. It's Dusty stuck up there not singing, with that plastic arm clutching her like a vice.

And when I try to sing the song without her I can't hear myself. I'm looking round for Philip, to join in and help me out, but I can't see him anywhere. There's only Alex, smoking and coughing up phlegm as usual, unbuttoning his shirt and scratching the scar on his throat to remind me I'm not quite on my own.

2

LYNN

Dr Lynn Arden, Senior Lecturer in Literary Linguistics, is about to run out of words. She does not know it yet, but this is where it is going to happen, on the first day of term, in the middle of a full lecture hall, in the company of the usual batch of recovering A-levellers; all of them the same as they were last year, as the year before that. She could tell you about the students with her eyes closed. They are still a week or so away from the racking cough of freshers' flu, their jeans have been washed within the last month, they are sporting clean A4 pads they look as if they intend to use. In acknowledgement of this effort, Lynn likes to present them with her prototype lecturer's persona on the first meeting. For this purpose she has chosen a dark suit, Liberty scarf, and applied her makeup (but not too much around the eyes) with her usual precision. Her style of delivery is clear, slightly informal, obviously experienced. The pale blonde hair, she knows, is not quite consistent with the prototype. Not so much the blondeness, more the aggressively platinum shade, out of date and context, an echo of a song stamped into vinyl that's never been digitally remastered. A colour she keeps up for a reason, or no reason, like a silver ring, a train ticket in an envelope. A bookmark poking from a book at the back of the desk, with the top bleached free of its design by years of sun.

So. The lecture for Week 1 locates the practice of language study, with which we are concerned this morning, within the context of a Postmodern world, a world where there are no longer any unities or artistic coherence, where authors are dead but won't lie down, and play, more or less entertainingly, in the sand, spitting salty mouthfuls now and again at the critical corpus. This well-rehearsed introduction is her favourite part, the part where she can taste bitterness like lemon pips on the tongue. The muttered conversation in the back row stops briefly, then resumes. A girl with pink hair asks if we haven't moved beyond the Postmodernist era. She gives an appropriately evasive answer.

All is as it should be, as it has been every September for the last ten years. I would ask you to look closely at the language you use, that we all use. Especially, I would ask you to think about *semantics,* the study of meaning. Is the meaning of a word single or multiple, does it move on or stand still? Does the word *spell* make you think of being placed under a curse, or just of a period of time? How would you decide which meaning the writer had intended? And what about the words associated with objects? Is a teddy bear warm and comforting or childish and irrelevant? Does a wedding ring mean stability or imprisonment? All your meanings are associations, *connotations*. And the associations you hold depend on where you are standing, on your past experience, on your history. Social, cultural, psychological background.

And so on, and so on. The mouse clicks and the images flash up in smooth succession. Teddy bear, bicycle, ice cream cone, red football, sandcastle, lipstick, razor, fridge, model, stiletto, medicine bottle, double bed, key, mirror, window. She has always resisted using pictures, but they get a better response than the words alone, a response that forgets the words are even there. And she's been doing this job long enough to know when the students are tired, when the contributions are drying up and it's time to stop. If only she could spare the time to listen there are a few interesting associations: an unmade double bed is a book left open, a window is a barred gate. A fridge is cryogenic suspension. A red football is God interceding in the affairs of man. She gives a tight smile that is meant to cover whatever irony is present, stops the presentation. Turns and looks at the clock.

Ten to eleven is what she expects to see, twenty to is what the hands are showing. There is a shortfall of ten minutes to be filled that she can't account for. Either she went too quickly through the material or she missed something out, left some of her notes at home. It's too late to ask for further contributions. They've moved on from the exercise, they're expecting something else from her. Any experienced lecturer can deal with this one: refer to the latest paper on psycholinguistics, relate an amusing anecdote. Use the reservoir of words accumulated during the long years of research. What Lynn does not yet realize is that there is no water in the reservoir.

She pauses, letting her voice run down into the silent murmur of a change of thought. What she might tell them, if the words would come, is that something has happened to her, something that she cannot explain rationally as she explains most of her experience. There is an envelope in her pocket, delivered in the post this morning, postmarked with the name of a seaside town she hasn't been back to in years. The envelope contains a key wrapped in a newspaper cutting. Not any key, not any cutting. She might hold these things up to them, as if they were only a metaphor, she might tell them that these things have meaning not to them, but only to her.

Not quite true, perhaps. But close enough.

But the words do not come.

The clock at the back of the lecture theatre ticks over a second minute of silence. It is odd enough now, sufficiently out of context, to be spreading to the students. They are looking at her, the girl with pink hair and the others. They look until she can feel herself becoming visible, as if she were dreaming of her clothes being peeled away, as other people do in dreams. She begins to panic, fighting for sayable words as if fighting for breath. Redundant metaphors, metaphors she has unpacked many times, rush into the void of her mind. She is a computer disk wiped clean, an amnesiac stumbling along a road. Despite the panic, her mind hears the metaphors as it has been trained to hear them, ready to split them into vehicle (the figurative, *untrue* term: she is a human being, not an item of computer software) and the tenor, the *true* meaning.

In the tenor is understanding, or so she has always believed. Only today there is no analysis, no understanding. No words.

But she knows that, however clumsily, she must speak and break the spell - *We'll leave it there* - and the students bundle their folders away and start to talk. A roar of their words rushes the ceiling like a swarm of bees, a black mass of words that are no use to her, that make her want to run from the hall with her hands flailing around her head. She is struck dumb, her tongue cloven to the roof of her mouth like someone or other in the Bible that she can no longer remember.

Her new office is permanently cold and, it seems, permanently nauseous with its walls of pale yellow and the smell of paint. The decorators have painted over the radiator pipes and the controls are stuck fast. She has no hope of discovering a set of spanners hidden beneath the pile of ancient floppy discs in her drawer and wrenching the valve into life so she sits in an old mohair cardigan drinking her mineral water and staring at the Staff Manual and Easter Days of Closure notices suspended like monochrome postmodernist flags from the pin board. These words will hold her together for the present, lift her clear of the ones she has glanced at, briefly only, in the newspaper cutting that lies firmly folded in her pocket; these short, sharp divisions of existence into Bank Holidays and procedures. Outside, the sun has finally got an eyelid over the green copper roof of the Senate Chamber across the courtyard and let carefully ruled lines of light through the venetian blind. A shadow, moving up and down, cuts across the lines occasionally. The slap of a spade hitting the ground follows each dip of the light. Someone is gardening in the herbaceous border outside.

Lynn gets up, makes a bow in the blind with a biro and looks out. A man in blue overalls is digging over the mixture of peaty soil and bark chippings ready for spring planting. A black and white collie (dogs are not allowed in the quad) is lying head on paws watching the movement of the spade. To the gardener's right is a Tesco plastic bag with a newspaper sticking out between its pricked handles. In front of the plastic bag, a red ball. Each time the spade is dug into the ground and left like a signpost with no direction the collie gets up and waits for the red ball to be rolled across the quad. The ball strikes the far kerb at satisfactory speed, rebounds; the collie barks and seizes it on the second bounce and the man squats down and waits for the ball to be dropped at his feet. Lynn notices how the blond fluff around the gardener's bald head is like a tidemark at ear-level, catching the sun, how his face is quiet in profile as if he has a secret and wonderful disability, like a deaf man at a football match.

God interceding in the affairs of man.

The sun flashes on her 40th-birthday present Rolex. She extricates the biro from the slats, allows the blind to snap back into place and sits down again. By some miracle of temporal mechanics the time has stuttered around to five past two. She gathers her papers, her whiteboard marker, water-bottle and keys, together. She will be late for the seminar hour for the first time in seven years. If anyone should ask - though no-one will - she will tell the truth, and say she has been watching an illicit ball-game in the quad. She will get away with this, but only as long as her words come back.

3.

In the middle of the night I wake up. I wake up because I know there are more dreams coming, dreams of things and people I don't recognize. Sometimes the dreams come like movies, but more often they're still, like photographs. There's a photo of a woman sitting on the end of a double bed, one of a flight of stairs with the light coming through a half-moon window at the top. One of a plastic windmill stuck in a sandcastle, one of a trail of red paint running down the centre of a road. To put off the time when I have to go back to sleep and look at these pictures I turn onto my back, lie very still and imagine I can hear the sound of Philip's breathing. He doesn't snore exactly, but his breath sounds as if he's breathing down very low, he rumbles into the pillow like a winter tide, the sort of tide that dredges up stones and branches and huge jellyfish, that leaves them high up on the beach and then retreats, far away, into the distance. Mostly I push his shoulder blade, very gently, but the rumbling doesn't stop and I don't want to wake him. Tonight I wait until I hear the car that always passes at five o'clock and then I get out of bed and stand at the window, peering through the gap in the curtains. The road outside is soil-brown under the streetlamps, faintly wet, silent. The real tide must be out, I can't hear it. Nothing and nobody is awake, except for me and the hotel on the other side of the road. The hotel is painted white, like most of the hotels in the town, but because it's built right at the end where the road meets the promenade, one side of it faces the seafront, the other looks across the road at the King's Head. A sort of turret room crowns the corner of the hotel, with curved walls and castellation on the roof. The room has two windows, one with a sea view and one without. Nobody ever stays in this room; nobody ever puts the lights on.

But downstairs, at ground floor level, the hotel bar is lit up and awake. It's an old-fashioned lounge with decor dating back to the Sixties, with black padded vinyl panels all round the bar and wicker furniture that must have been brought in later, in the seventies. There are fluorescent lights in the ceiling and green lights behind the bar that illuminate all the bottles on the optics and the shelves. The light's too much for the room, it overflows into the street all night; it lies on the tarmac like a dull orange wave. The bulbs are burning their energy away, waiting for someone to come and turn them off. I can feel the heat of them, it burns my skin like sand.

I want to shut my eyes, but I have to keep on looking. If I stare for long enough I know that somebody will come in. While I'm waiting I imagine the rest of the room, I notice the squashed cushions on the chairs and the drinks left behind from the night before, the empty beer-glasses and the half-drunk Guinness. A bottle that looks a bit like a Coke bottle, only it's half-full of a turquoise blue liquid, I don't know the name of the drink, but the colour is like the colour of the sea when you're walking on the road around the headland, a colour that's really the sun's rays mixed with something in the water. Beside the bottle there's a glass tankard with a handle, full to the brim with a thick dark green drink. I know the name of this drink, it's Crème de Menthe, sweet and thick and stains your teeth. A woman's drink.

The door to the lounge opens and a man comes in. He has black Brylcreemed hair and a pipe in his mouth; he carries a newspaper and some other papers under his arm. A big man, wearing a dark tweed suit with heavy shoulders, a Forties suit. He sits down at a chair in the window with his back to me, puts the newspaper on the table and takes a fountain pen from a pocket in his jacket. He starts to write on the loose papers, tapping the pen down the paper as if he's adding up figures. The bottle with the blue liquid and the Crème de Menthe are both on the table but he doesn't seem to see the blue drink, it's the Crème de Menthe he moves to the edge of the table, clearing the centre to make more space for his writing.

The Brylcreem man writes for a long time. He's waiting for me to remember who he is, but he won't wait for ever. Once the door opens again and the barman comes in to clear up he'll disappear. And loneliness will knock me off my feet like a wave.

In the morning the lights are out, and Philip's not there. Before he left, last Tuesday, he gave me some money to go shopping.

'Get yourself some of that yellow perfume,' he said. 'Then you can spray it round the room to keep the blues away.'

I fold the notes carefully and put them with the others in my tapestry bag. When I get back to the pub I tuck the shopping bag underneath my seat, and put my feet together in front of it. The bottle is safely held inside its pieces of white moulded plastic, inside its yellow box, its white plastic bag. I'll leave it there, unopened, as long as I possibly can. Filling the glass, Megan, Jerry will say when he sees it. Filling the glass.

But tonight Jerry doesn't come. There's just his bar-stool with its red plush seat and the beer mat wedged under one leg to keep it steady, and beyond that the copper corner of the bar and the pale top halves of the faces of the people on the seat near the door, faces I don't usually have to see because of Jerry's check shirt and the three folds of skin where his head meets his neck and his clipped brown skull getting in the way.

One of the faces has a hat shadowing its eyes. A blue velvet hat, the sort they used to call a Fedora. The Fedora is just one in Alex's collection of hats, but it's a favourite, and in a moment he'll come over and sit with me and start talking about the old times. Because Jerry isn't there I can see him getting up, stubbing his cigarette out on the empty crisp packet in the ashtray, tilting the blue hat back on his head. He looks across at me with his dark blue eyes staring out of his raw-pastry skin, his eyebrows permanently raised, not in surprise but in something more and less childish. Alex wears a worn-out 70s brown suede jacket that suits him somehow, it looks like the inside of his skin worn outside, with all the scratches and red stains on view for everyone to see. And his hands are like x-ray hands. So thin, there's something not quite right about them being wrapped around a pint of Guinness. It's one of those jokes where nobody laughs.

But the weak can always spot someone weaker than themselves, they've got the inside knowledge for it. Alex straddles the stool opposite me and lights another cigarette before leaving it burning in the ashtray, grey and crumbling and smoking by itself; and smiles at me, showing the standing stones of three teeth in his lower jaw.

'Sad eyes again, Megan,' he croaks.

I nod and push the bag further underneath the seat. He's seen it though, his eyes are like crabs' eyes, they swivel; they never miss a trick.

Alex has a slug of Guinness.

'Ash Wednesday,' he says, and looks at me to see if I'm going to laugh.

'Let's do the day we met,' he says, and so we do.

Alex remembers things. He remembers things, not from a distance but close-to, as if he was inside them. Once he told me memory was just like a bus trip round the headland, it depends if you're on the bus or chasing after it and watching it get further and further away. When you're sitting on the bus you can look out to sea, down to the beach, up to the church and the lighthouse and the graveyard, you can see anything you want. But when you're chasing all you see is the bus disappearing round a corner.

Sometimes in my dreams I'm on the bus. But mostly it takes Alex talking and talking, scraping away at me like sandpaper, to get me there.

So we do the day we met. And for a while I'm back at Sapphire tidying the racks and putting clear plastic covers over vintage evening dresses, sorting the new clothes into piles ready for Betty to price, when I suddenly spot Alex's white sunhat poking out from among the old fur coats on the rail at the back of the shop. I would never have seen him if it hadn't been for the hat; he'd tucked himself away with the brown glossy animal skins like a hibernating hedgehog. Fancied a fur coat for the winter season, he said when I found him. And I didn't know what he meant about the winter season, so he sang a few bars of Misty for me in a kind of thin falsetto, but perfectly in tune.

Lucky for him it was Betty's day off, I said, but by then I'd recognized him from the poster in the Amusement Arcade. *Every Sunday at eight*, it said, *a new sensation from the Emerald Isle* above a picture of Alex in full flow, his mouth stretched open like a letterbox, angel hair in a thick fringe and shadows under hung over eyes, looking the way a singer was supposed to look. When he emerged from the racks at Sapphire in the flesh, you couldn't see where his hair ended and the fur began. It had to be fox, he said,

24

because it went so well with his colouring, it was the best fiver he ever spent. On cabaret nights he'd walk down to the Pier Head Bar wearing the coat with a storm force westerly whipping up his skirts, and wintry breakers firing up spray over the pier till the salt sparkled like stars on the fur. And Alex being Alex, he still wore the coat even after some Animal Rights protesters threw paint over him in the middle of Smoke Gets in Your Eyes. Philip said he looked like a Beauty Without Cruelty campaign ad, getting up on stage like a shrunken dowager with a splash of red all down his back, but nobody ever bothered him again about wearing fur.

I wonder where the coat is now, I wonder if he sleeps wrapped up in it in shop doorways on cold nights, but I don't ask. I don't mention anything that happens after closing time, in case he isn't there when Ralph unlocks in the morning.

Only I miss his voice, his soft sweet voice. It was that or his life, Dearie, Olive said, No contest. But I don't know. I don't know.

'Still a Sapphire girl,' he croaks, rooting round my feet, pulling out my carrier bag and bringing out the yellow box with the perfume in it. He tears the cellophane off, opens the box and takes the perfume from its plastic bed and sprays some onto his suede lapel. The perfume leaves a dark wet patch like a hole in the jacket. I don't complain, don't say a word. I can't take my eyes off it.

He looks round the pub.

'No sign of him,' he says, and looks back at me.

I shake my head.

Alex sniffs at the wet patch.

'Old smell,' he says. 'Out of fashion.'

I start to say I don't care but he interrupts me and stares at me again.

'Been gone a long time,' he says. 'Too long. Time to stop waiting.'

I don't answer. I turn away from him and sip at my drink until it steadies the shivers in my stomach.

'Music time!' Alex says suddenly, and takes off again, scattering customers right and left and cadging round the regulars for 50p.

It's only when I look through the gap he's made I see that the jukebox is dark. It's switched off.

'Leave it, Alex,' I say. 'Leave it.'

He isn't listening. He's scrabbling on the floor with the plug in his hand trying to find the socket, getting up again and cursing, with his Fedora shoved to the back of his head and wisps of sandy hair escaping from the brim and standing up with static, yelling for Ralph as he wrestles with the flex.

But Ralph doesn't work the bar on Wednesdays, he's in the back doing whatever it is he does in there, and nobody bothers him unless it's urgent, a fight or the brewery or a dodgy twenty pound note. Alex is leaning on the bar croaking out Ralph's name like a bony old frog, his brown suede jacket knocking empties from the bar as he waves his arms. And Ralph emerges from the back, his arms folded and his face smudged with stubble, letting Alex rant for a minute and then looking past him, through the space he's cut through the regulars, straight at me. Stands tipped back on his heels and looks at me, sort of taken aback, as if I was some old wallpaper he found under the anaglypta while he was stripping down a wall. Paper with swirls in pink and orange that make your eyes ache, some old pattern he can't believe is still there. And he'll shake his head at it for a minute, but then it's the scraper out again. Down to the bare wall, where there's just old paste and whitewash and a few

26

numbers scribbled God knows when in pencil or some shaky capital letters nobody can understand.

'Shut it,' he says to Alex, still looking across the space. 'Shut it, or you're barred.'

'We need our music, Ralph,' says Alex, sliding from the bar, slewing round and looking at me. 'Megan needs her music.'

'I'll give you music, you bloody little tramp. And you can both of you stand outside the door and listen to it.'

I freeze, the way I do when Philip's angry, but it's too late for that. Ralph is remembering I'm there, the way he hasn't remembered for years, not since the old days when he first came to the King's Head and inherited me along with the pub. When he had a dark beard and frizzy hair and it was Pauline with her laugh and her jangling bracelets who was behind the bar, night after night. He's made a note in his head and it'll be the scraper out after closing time, after Alex has staggered off to the night shelter with as many cans as he can hide in his sticky pockets. I know it.

Except he isn't going to wait till closing time. He wipes his hands on the glass towel and swings it onto his shoulder, letting it tip forward against my hair as he gets astride the stool Alex has abandoned. He raises his eyebrows to focus on me with the wrinkles on his forehead rippling up and breaking on his crew-cut. A word in your ear, Megan. About the refurbishment, some things need to know. Only it's going to be a word next week, when it suits him. Refurbishment. He likes all those syllables, I can see that. Even better he likes making me wait, wondering what he's going to say, what he'll send crashing round my ears.

I know it. Memory never did me any good.

4

A name has come to Lynn in her dreams, a name she hasn't used for years. It glows in the dark like the key on the table beside her bed. She lies on her side with her head on her outstretched arm and watches the clock click over from one minute to the next. The figures stare back at her and rearrange their dashes into new numbers precisely every sixty seconds. And slowly the room resolves itself into a series of firmly drawn shapes, just being solid, standing guard as a house should do.

Only when the shapes are steady can she remember which house she's in. This is the third she's occupied since her appointment. The first was a Victorian terrace in a quiet, university-dormitory type street, a thin-fronted house recently vacated by a History lecturer taking early retirement. She had applied just at the right time, the Accommodation Office said, and she took the house without even viewing it, because who knew when another one would come up? The History lecturer, who she never saw, left behind his damp carpets and William Morris Acanthus curtains, neither of which would lose the smell of Nut Brown. And most of his furniture, which she was glad of until she began to unearth various miscellaneous pieces of paper from the three-piece suite while cleaning: apparently innocuous notes like shopping lists, references to academic journals, lists of numbers. She bought a tasselled ecru throw to cover up the sofa and piled the notes under a beach pebble on the coffee table, but she couldn't leave the lists alone, trying to find a code in them, some correspondence of numbers to letters that she could make sense of.

She felt as if she'd seen the lecturer's handwriting, or something like it, many times. The writing was typically academic: abrupt figures and letters that were never joined together but jabbed at the paper like knife-marks. While trying to decipher the code for the fourth time, she realized that the numbers were arranged in two columns, and that each pair of numbers added up to 21. 13 and 8, 10 and 11, 4 and 17. After that she left the lists alone, and replaced them under their pebble; but over the weeks while she was settling in to her new job, she became steadily more convinced that the History lecturer had committed suicide. Nobody said so, of course, nor did she expect them to. *Early retirement* was simply part of another code, one that was not for cracking, but learning. In those days she was ready to do that.

But after a couple of months the Nut Brown and the numbers on the coffee table got too much for her and she took a flat on campus. There the furniture was clean and new and chilly, and all trace of previous occupants had been swept away before she moved in. The worst of it was that her rooms were at the end of the corridor right next to the payphone. She was billeted with postgraduates, of course, but they seemed to spend their evenings calling Kuala Lumpur and Beijing and Nairobi in loud, permanently excited voices, and always in languages where the consonants and vowels ran together into expressive, painful sounds, like bows sawing violins or heavy hands crashing down onto an untuned piano. Curiously, perhaps, she never stopped her ears. Instead she acquired the habit of listening without understanding; emotional listening, she called it to herself for no particular reason; except that there was no emotion, or rather the emotion was outside in the corridor, firmly locked out behind the door. The noise it made filled her head like static, a static of sounds with no words in it. Whenever the noise stopped, her brain threw up words at her: sheets, wine, sandcastle, ribbon, stiletto, teddy-bear, sea; and she would pace the edges of the hearthrug, trying to force them out with other words. Papers, account, signature, clearance.

But at work she never needed any of those words. Speech between colleagues in the department was formal, English for Academic Purposes, otherwise known as EAP.

'Anything that can be reduced to an acronym will be,' as a cheerful Scottish professor told her after the second glass of wine at a staff lunch. 'Keeps the bastards guessing.'

And she laughed with her fellow diners, but it was her laughter that drained away first. For a while, she attempted to talk monographs and research grants with the best of them, only (to her ear at least) there was always a rising inflexion in her voice that gave her away, as if she had picked up the language phonetically, like Bela Lugosi learning English in order to play Dracula; uttering the sounds, disconnected from their meaning.

Once or twice she toyed with the idea of asking the Scottish professor and some of his cronies back to the flat to get disgustingly drunk and indulge in a mutual shedding of EAP and research, but when she assessed the flat as a social venue she lost her nerve. The long low beige sofa would seat three, four at a pinch, four more on the pale ash dining chairs, a couple maybe on the mock-Persian hearthrug. But the flat was a place where nobody lived. There was nothing to look at, nothing to talk about; no paintings on the walls, no photographs of graduations or ex-husbands or estranged children. Only tickets to a guest lecture on the mantelpiece, only a vase of white and mauve silk chrysanthemums on the windowsill; and, looking self-conscious on the coffee table, the latest Margaret Atwood and a Philip Larkin collection, one of which she was reading (for metaphorical content rather than pleasure) when she remembered to. No clues, not so much as a spooky list of numbers to engage the left side of the brain. A drinks party here would be like a gathering in a railway station waiting-room, a pause between destinations, a place for people in transit. People who avoid meeting one another's eyes, who give nothing away.

Of course she could have unpacked the six cardboard boxes stacked in the bedroom and labelled in black dry-marker pen *Arden, The Round House*; draped herself and her life around the room, but she wouldn't unpack because she didn't intend to stay. As soon as another small Victorian terrace appeared on the market she waited only long enough to check that the departing tenant had no academic connections before snapping it up. Then she moved on again, with her books and cardboard boxes and the lecturer's list of numbers slipped in to the front of a file.

To this house, the third house. And now it's time to move on again, or back. She doesn't know which. The key is still glowing, but fainter now, as if the light behind has been burning too long, as if it's fading out.

Eventually she gets out of bed, goes into the bathroom to turn on the shower, leaves it running while she walks around the upstairs bedrooms. The cold tinny sound of the water follows her around. She wanders in and out of the rooms, staring at their contents as if she has been away for a long time, as if she was an estate agent. Bedroom 1, fitted white units floor to ceiling, grey and lilac decorations, pale laminate flooring. Bedroom 2, office. Beech effect desk, PC, pin-boards with year planner, postcards of mountain views, pennants from American colleges. Miscellaneous cupboards, books, books, books. Bedroom 3, store.

Undusted shelves with empty vases, pot-plants needing watering, six cardboard boxes labelled Arden, The Round House. A large green metal trunk, no label.

She goes to the topmost box of the first stack of three, pulls the interwoven flaps apart, and takes out a pile of postcards held together by a rubber band. She pulls out a card and looks at it. A view of the seaside, no more and no less remarkable than any other such view. The greenish-blue sea which occupies most of the centre of the picture is framed by two buildings, one either side of a road that terminates on the seafront. On the left, an indeterminate structure that might be flats or the side wall of a pub; the corner of a white-painted hotel on the right. The hotel is of the late Victorian period, the heyday of the building of seaside hotels; it has three visible floors with a turret-type room built on to the corner of the highest, topped by a conical green slate roof. The turret room seems to lean out from the masonry of the hotel into the backcloth of sea like a boat heading out from land or the figurehead on a ship.

In the empty centre of the picture, the road ends in a broad expanse of promenade. Frozen figures, children, dogs, small dark squares of pushchairs and wheelchairs, dot the grey concrete. Dead-centre of the promenade, and photograph, a tall white obelisk points skywards, its stepped marble base cordoned off from the public by dark posts and a chain-link fence. Around the steps, the faint red circles of poppy-day wreaths are just visible.

Lynn turns the card over, but there is no handwritten message on the back. She tries to construct one: *Having a splendid time*, *Wish you were here*; but there's another message writing itself across the card, in handwriting very different from the History lecturer's: strong, black letters scored into the paper, pressing on the picture on the other side. She can see his name, rolling through her mind, forming its expansive, unmistakable signature: *Phil*. She flips the card over again, replaces it in the bundle and drops it back into its place in the box, re-plaits the cardboard flaps, and goes and sits on the landing with her back against the banisters and her eyes closed. The water is still pouring. The sound of it makes the house feel as if it's not solid at all, but a soft house, a house with no walls, or rather walls that melt when you lean on them. Or maybe it's her that's soft with no edges. She looks at her fingers, perfectly manicured and curling inward towards the palms of her hands, the hands a foot or so apart, propped on her knees. Holding something round, with no edges.

It was a red ball. God interceding in the affairs of Man.

'Jesus Christ,' she says to the ceiling. 'Go and do something.'

She drags herself up and goes into the bathroom, hangs her bathrobe on the hook and kicks off her white towelling slippers. Just before she gets into the cubicle, she pushes the door to behind her.

After a few seconds there is a cry. Not a domestic, everyday, fallen-on-the-soap kind of yelp, but a full-blown, stretched out wail, echoing and stretching, the cry of someone fallen down a disused well, a mine-shaft, a hole that slips into other holes, deeper and deeper with no full moon of daylight above it. A snake of a tunnel burrowing into soil and then rock, relentlessly down, where it should be colder.

The sound coming from the bathroom changes from a cry to crying, the sort children do when they want you to know that they're in distress. Inside, Lynn is holding the palms of her hands against red shoulders, rocking herself to and fro on the white tiled floor. In her mind the picture of the seafront has reappeared, only this time the turret sits square in the centre of the frame, blocking out the obelisk.

The sun flashes off its upstairs windows like Morse code frozen in a burst of light. Part of a word, part of a letter, she can't tell but she can. Her crying has words in it, if anyone could hear them, the kind of words that children say through tears because they haven't yet learned that crying and words are two separate things.

Just because the water was red-hot. Red-hot, when she was expecting it to be cold.

5.

I see the change in Ralph's face when he's ready to talk to me. I've seen it before, when there are bikers to throw out or stroppy bar staff to fire. There's a dark tinge to his skin, a kind of five o'clock shadow, not just round the chin but the eyes too. He knows it's there, he keeps rubbing at it with his fingers as if he's getting ready to shave it away. Your skin remembers the beard, I say to him when I've had a few, but I won't be saying it today. Because it's not closing time, but opening time on a Tuesday morning. Jerry's still in the bookies, Olive's out with her flowered straw basket prodding all the fruit down at the market and not buying any, Alex won't even surface for another couple of hours. I'm sitting at my corner table with the sunlight coming through the baffle glass window and shining off the copper tabletop and my tranny's on, playing Classic Gold very quietly, not bothering anybody. The Trems are into the second chorus of Silence is Golden, and I'm mouthing the words with them. And my nails are wet. Wet with Pink Champagne polish which has bits of silver glitter in it. The second coat is on and my hands are flat on the table. I have to keep them still.

Ralph sits himself down in the way of the sunlight and talks. The tranny stays on, but the signal fades, or it sinks under the sound of that voice hitting the air like a fist against the wall. And for a while the talk flows over me. It's all about new upholstery, and tables with brass numbers on them, and shelves full of green bottles and woodworking tools and advertising signs for Colman's mustard, and a blackboard offering paninis and baguettes and Chicken

Tikka. The words clog my brain like leftover food in a sink that won't go down. I see the bar filling up with objects so you can't even walk across the room without stepping over cardboard boxes full of the things that are being thrown away. The things he doesn't have the space for any more. And I know what's coming. I don't even ask about the jukebox.

He rubs his chin and the dark doesn't come off. In his mind he's finished the bar, carpeted the floor, he's moving on through the pub. The door marked Private is gone. It's replaced by a pseudo-Victorian door with a cloudy glass panel that has scrolling patterns round the edges. And written in the very centre of the panel, clear letters in the frosted glass, isn't Private, but Apartments. Or Guest Rooms. Ralph hasn't decided, but the brewery says he can do either. And he's thinking about it, he's through the door and coming up the stairs. I can hear the greasy treads sucking at his trainers.

'Then there's number four,' he says.

My number. Alex says he'd have put a fiver on me choosing an odd number over an even one, but four's my favourite. It's got a neatness that calms me down when Philip's late and I'm drinking too much. Four numbers, four letters. And Ralph knows I chose it, he knows it's the last room in the house, the one you get to when the landing's running out, when the wall at the end's rushing up to meet you and the only alternative is the right turn into my room. Last turn, last room.

He didn't knock the first time either. Opening doors right and left as if he was already the landlord, and Pauline dragging along behind him with her bracelets jangling. He never could go anywhere with her without everyone knowing who was coming, he hated her for it in the end. I was sitting up in bed with my tea spilt all down the quilt, and there was Ralph with his beard and Afro standing stock-still in the doorway with the door wide open.

'Oh,' he said, with his hand closed on the doorknob. 'This one's occupied.'

Then he started laughing.

Pauline jangled up to him and put her head round his shoulder.

'Sorry, love,' she said. 'He was brought up in a market. Not used to doors.'

I liked Pauline's voice as soon as I heard it. It was singsong Welsh, all the words ending in an upstroke. And Ralph didn't say anything, but he got the door and shoved her back onto the landing with it. She swore at him but he got the door shut, with her behind it. And then he was inside. If I'd been on my own in the room that day he'd have swept me away then and there, bundled me out the back with the bins in my lilac eiderdown. Only Philip was leaning on the windowsill having a cigarette and he turned round in his white Nehru jacket and his black shirt and just zapped Ralph with his eyes like a laser rifle with one of those blue hard beams that look hot ice. *Will you get the hell out of here.* Not even a question, he didn't do questions in those days. I loved that.

But now Philip isn't here. And Ralph's saying that number four isn't going to be number four any more, it's going to be knocked into the room next door to make a suite, it won't have a number but a name, a name he isn't telling me about because it won't be mine. And now he's close to me, so close that he isn't coming through the door any more, he's watching while the builders crash through the wall with a sledgehammer, leaving a hole like a cave-mouth. There's wallpaper weeping off the walls and grey veins of wiring hanging from the ceiling, hanging down from the broken wall and spitting sparks onto the red brick sand on the floor. But worst of all I can see into the room next door, into number three. And it's still neat, none of the rubble has fallen that way. I thought the last lodger had moved out, I thought I was the only one left, but inside there's a new white carpet and bleached wood chairs round a long table. A big mirror over a marble fireplace. From where I'm standing the mirror reflects the room but if I went through the hole it would reflect something else. Me, or whoever owns the room, I don't know. I go close to the hole and touch one of the bricks and it goes back to sand in my fingers. The wiring flashes on and off like broken Christmas lights, all one colour. And I can't go through. The panic rises up my body, a sneeze that won't blow outward but sucks itself back into me, like the rubble round my feet.

Ralph's said his piece, and he doesn't want to stay around for the aftershock. As he swings his leg over the stool I think he says something about the end of the month. Which month, I want to ask, but the words won't reach my mouth. Because in my throat it's years, years, years.

Only my hands haven't betrayed me, they're flat and still on the table as I left them. I try the varnish on my left hand with my right index finger. It's dry and smooth and gleams in the sunlight. But the bits of glitter are rough and gritty, I can feel them through the polish. Like grains of sand.

I turn round and look behind me at the door marked Private. The door is shimmering, coming and going with the sunlight. I have to get through before it disappears, get myself up the stairs to the dirty black payphone to ring Philip's mobile. Three fours, two sevens, five zeros and a two, not in that order. A female voice answers and tells me that the phone is switched off but she doesn't say if you can leave a message on a mobile and I can't remember. So I keep on ringing, right through the day, with the grease on the earpiece sticking to my hair and the mouthpiece held away from my mouth and the message repeating over and over again, as if I was throwing my voice.

Each time I ring I feel more hopeless, more as if I'm fading into the distance. And my voice fades with me, dissipates in the air on the landing. I'm outside, alone, in the dark.

6.

Lynn flicks the light on and walks up to the mirror. If there was someone else in the Ladies she would bend over the basins and check for shine, neaten the line of her lipstick, comb the fringe back over her forehead. Since there is nobody, she hesitates, looking round as if she has been found out in some illicit act: smoking, sex, or some kind of unhealthy self-regard that only she can diagnose. She has always had trouble with mirrors. Even those that were scarcely mirrors at all, the sort little girls were given to hold, with pink plastic scrolling handles and the oval of glass slightly opaque, more solid than reflective, like toffee. She understood at an early age that you did not really look in such mirrors but carried them jealously, like a lapel-badge of office or devotion, a sign to the world of the self you would become. Later, the mirrors changed, but the face would slip sideways, leave the room so that the reflection remained elusive. A mirror in the school toilets showed a half-face looking over a shoulder, a bees' nest of pale glued hair; and, just above the shoulder, beside the face but not clearly belonging to it, there was a hand holding a lighted cigarette, a hand gesturing upward.

Later still there was another hand, seen in an antique mirror hung over a fireplace: a mirror that had nothing to do with reflection, a grotesque ornament ready to haul the plaster from the walls with sheer tonnage of gilded glass and framework. If she tries to focus on it now, at this distance of time, she sees a golden yellow duster sweeping back and forth across the glass like an exotic jellyfish in a

40

tank, and a hand with a silver bracelet under it, a bracelet that must be hers because of the tinkle of the charms.

But she cannot be sure about what she remembers. Too much of it is laced with the metaphors she no longer trusts, too much is undermined by the propensity of mirrors to distort. Once she invariably saw in them what was not there, gazing into the glass for some missing part of her reflection; just as a child she would look at the displays in shoe-shops and wonder why there were only single shoes for sale. And always, her mind would go inside the shop, down a narrow flight of stairs into the stockroom, where each shoe's unworn pair was hidden inside a closed box, wrapped in black tissue paper, in some way not a pair for the one upstairs at all.

It is years ago. And the shoe in the box, which she never saw, is still more real than the one on display.

She gives herself a little shake, checks her watch and turns away from the mirror. The appointment she has requested with her Head of Department is in five minutes' time. As a therapist might say to her, it is time to talk, to explain that her words have not come back, that she can no longer do her job. She still understands, she can still make them understand; but now there is a silence standing behind her when she speaks, a silence that is stronger than her words, her explanations. It is as if a hole has been punched through the centre of her life, and through it she sees the life that has lain underneath it for years glinting up at her, demanding that she look at it. She wants to tell herself, as she would tell her students, that she cannot even think about this hole, or void, or absence, or whatever it is, without first giving it a name, a linguistic signifier, but this is another of the theories in which she no longer believes. Something is there in the silence which cannot be expressed; but it is as solid as the man in the quad with the black and white collie.

But these are not the things she will say. She will tell Richard, the Head of Department, merely that she needs a break. All time away from teaching, as she knows before she asks, must be to do with words: an unfinished book, a series of articles, a lucrative editorship which will reflect well on the university. She will be vague, use an old proposal for research found in her office drawer. She will mention fieldwork, more work on metaphor in everyday life. Above all, she will not tell the truth. The truth would be an uncomfortable pause to Richard, with his beige hair and sagging bookshelves and his gaze fixed eternally six inches to the left of her face.

She is about to knock on Richard's door when she hears a voice in her head, a voice that is not hers but, undeniably, Phil's Transatlantic twang; a sound that reached her, like the signal from a distant galaxy, before his words ever came.

She knocks twice on the door, hears the response *Come in* and takes a step backward. Of course, she has forgotten. The words always came first.

Richard's room is on the ground floor of the oldest building in the university, a large sunlit personal library which he has hung on to for a decade. This extended occupation is no mean feat in a time of Faculty reorganization, but Richard is an academic of the old school. His gown still hangs behind the door, his lectures are delivered impromptu, he sleeps inoffensively through the few Staff Meetings he attends. His room is well-defended against School Managers and Efficiency Reviews, a research-lined bunker where books reach to the ceiling on three of the four walls, dark brown shelves separating them into strata, pressing them like wine as the years pass, covering them with dust and encrustation.

In the centre of the room is a table whose surface is entirely covered by various piles of papers, essays, monographs and correspondence, each pile paper-weighted by a large pebble. Four elderly dining chairs surround the table, but Lynn is sitting in a privileged position, in one of the two easy chairs underneath the window. Although 'easy' is probably the wrong epithet, because the springing in the chairs perished long ago, and the seat cushion is lumpy and faintly malodorous, like an old mattress, hollowed and peaked by the shapes of other bodies, making her shift her weight uneasily from side to side.

Richard is on the phone to somebody in Cambridge, obliging her to wait, and still she does not know which words will break out of her. On her knee, as a prompt, is a printout of the email she sent him yesterday. The email is brief and succinct. It requests a month's leave for personal reasons, temporary teaching cover, and (unexpectedly) an opportunity to speak with him personally. From Richard's half of the telephone conversation, she gathers that the matter of her replacement is already settled. Dr Kathryn Noble of Corpus, research specialism Historical Linguistics. Not, perhaps, a perfect match for Lynn's modules in contemporary discourse, but a like-minded colleague with whom Richard can debate etymologies *ad nauseam* in the Staff Club.

Lynn moves her tongue slightly in her mouth. It feels dry, heavy, toxic as mercury. She can hear the girl with pink hair challenging her, over and over again, in that plaintive, irritating little-girl voice, saying she doesn't believe that *language* and *tongue* are really synonyms.

43

Your textbook says so, she answers wearily, therefore they are.

But do you believe it, Dr Arden? she says.

Ruthie. The girl's name is Ruthie.

The view from Richard's window is not of the quad but a pleasing vista down a grassy bank to the lake. The water is flat and unmoving, like a sheet of ice. Out in the centre of the lake two swans arch their wings and attempt to defend a scrap of island from a noisy group of Canada geese. Lynn hates the lake, hates its grey metallic surface and the green scum that beads its dirty margins. Dead water, she used to say to Phil, something you'll never understand unless you were raised by the sea. And mostly when she said this Phil would shrug his shoulders and light another Consulate, but this time he bends over and says in her ear

So what the hell happened in the lecture, dumb-ass?

They're walking side by side, the way they used to when she was an undergraduate and showing him off to her friends, doing the circuit of the lake. She takes the cigarette from Phil's hand and does the slow exaggerated shaking of her head that means, I don't know, I can't explain, that speaks her dumbness more heavily than the words can. Remember, only seven per cent of communication is verbal. The other ninety three per cent is gesture, action, tone of voice.

Should help you out, then, if you've forgotten how to talk.

They start walking again. Always clockwise, with the iron railings on their right, the building with the white tower on the grassy hill the other side of the lake. The lunchtime circuit, along with all the other academics, some of them in deep discussion, some perched on benches, fighting their way into plastic triangles of sandwich. Round and round, round and round.

Dead water, she says, and makes to take Phil's arm. He turns and fixes her with a cold blue gaze and she says

Why come back now?

At that precise moment he disappears, and the lake recedes back behind the window. She feels herself shaking. Underneath her the seat shifts, pitches like a pleasure boat in a heavy swell. Richard has settled himself in the chair opposite her, his legs crossed, or rather twined around one another, his limbs thin and flexible and tough as rope. As he peers at his own annotated printout of Lynn's message his head with its long beige hair nods slightly. There is an impression of fatigue about him, one that he has been cultivating for years, and only an address in the right language will dispel it. A question on semiotics would do the trick, an acerbic comment on other people's glossaries.

Throw a stone in, dumb-ass, says Phil's disembodied voice.

She looks over at the table with its mounds of papers, each with its summit pebble. Her tongue is heavy as the stones, darker, not connected with the whiteness in her head, the place where language used to be. Something else, something that can't remember its own name. She starts to get up, her legs shaking, as if she has been ill. Richard jumps with the unexpected movement and splutters into speech, adjusting his glasses and squinting at his notes. As Lynn may have heard, Dr Noble is only too happy to step into the breach. There will be some forms to sign, and Margaret will be writing to her about the details, but no need to come in to the office. In due course, she can email him with an update on her situation. She has got to the door before he looks up, fixes his gaze six inches to the left of her face and says

'Was there anything else?'

45

Lynn moves her head slowly to the right. She feels her mouth opening, forming around the vowel of *No*, she hears the sound emerging from it, a sound shattering the whiteness, as if she were breaking down her own bathroom door. A strange half of a word coming out of her without the consonant, the sound jerking Richard's head back towards her, his expression one of comical alarm, the alarm of a man who finds his nose pushed unexpectedly against the window of female emotions.

'Yes,' she says. 'There is something.'

She walks back into the room, stands behind the easy chair, digs her fingernails into its noxious upholstery.

'My personal tutees,' she says. 'One girl in particular is in need of extra support.'

Richard sinks back down in his chair, his head nodding gently, muttering something about the Counselling Service. He will make a note immediately.

'Ruthie,' says Lynn. 'Her name is Ruthie.'

For the second time she turns to go, stops at the door. The mounds of paper rise like hills between them.

'She has pink hair. And she sleepwalks.'

What's wrong with now? Phil says in her ear as she goes back down the corridor, lets herself in to her office, leans back against the cold yellow radiator.

You were dead to me already. I don't need to read about you in the papers.

Not a bad review, all told, he says.

So what do you want?

She waits and listens a moment longer, but he's gone. She turns and peers out through the blind, but the quad too is empty. She lets down the slats to the sill, closes them tight against the daylight, checks the drawers, carefully removes her office key from her key ring and places it on the desk. Her phone rings four times and the answering message kicks in. Lynn hears her voice saying she isn't there, the long tone, the silence afterwards. She flinches, and then she is out of the office, letting the door swing behind her.

The departmental corridor stretches in front of her, doors shut on either side all the way down to the swing doors at the end. Her footsteps are loud, with the impact of her high black heels on the polished floor, but - it is probably her imagination - the rhythm of the footfall is unbalanced, limping, with the dragging of the phantom shoe. She can't guess who the footsteps belong to. Much less, where they're going.

7

One Tuesday passes, then another Tuesday. Philip doesn't come. Now when I ring his mobile there isn't an answering voice there at all, just a long hard note that holds and then stops and then silence. Not silence for a message, a silence to drive me away, a silence to make me give in. Alex doesn't help, he tries to talk me out of trying, he comes upstairs with me and pulls at the cord when I'm dialing, as if he's going to pull it from the wall. Downstairs in the pub, Jerry's back on his bar stool scratching the stubble on the back of his neck and he says Don't worry, the man's got himself a new phone, he'll be in touch; but Olive squeezes my arm with her Purple Haze fingernails digging in to my flesh and shakes her head.

'Let it go, poppet,' she says, and when she says this I look down at my feet. I want to tell her that I'd like to talk, but Philip's made the silence and I can't undo it. If I try to talk the words won't come out right, they'll be broken up in pieces too small for anyone to understand. The pub floorboards will open up and under them I'll see the stony beach below the headland, with the broken rocks where the cormorants and shags perch to dry their wings.

Olive takes her talons out and looks at me and digs around in her basket.

'Why don't you go and see the little mite and tell her all about it,' she says. 'Take her a flower.'

The flower is an old poppy that Olive sometimes wears on Remembrance Day. It's a car poppy, a bit dusty, but I take it anyway. I get on the little vintage bus that takes tourists on trips round the headland and go to visit Quetzal.

For days it's been raining, and when I get off the bus near the summit and go through the iron gate and up the grass path into the churchyard the wet ground sags under my feet, it's like walking through the soft sand on the beach, soft sand letting you down into the sea.

The graveyard is a huge one, white and black and grey stones spilling out over the slope of the headland from almost the summit right down to the road. Nearest the church are the real graves, with white angels like Quetzal in flowing robes and wings held upward like a swan's and hands held together in prayer. Most of the angels are on very old graves with nobody left to remember them, but they're not lonely, they have one another, they stand with their wings against the wind and their beautiful faces turned away from the salty air, their hair white and curling in the mist.

Quetzal's angel is further out, though, on her own with the rows of modern graves, black dead slabs of marble, where there are words but no faces and no voices. She hates it there, so I talk to her as often as I can. Because of Philip I haven't been for a couple of weeks but the presents will have made her happy, they'll last until I can get to her.

The graveyard is on the side of the headland sheltered from the worst of the wind, but Quetzal's hanky has still blown off the grave and got plastered by the rain onto a stone a couple of graves away. As I walk through the long grass to get it back I can see the embroidered initial facing me like a mouth, a wet green mouth coming up for air. I peel the hanky from the stone, fold it up again and place it safely underneath the vase. The soap is still where I left it, but water has got inside the plastic and made the soap a soft lilac mass, like plasticine.

The necklace with the red stones has gone. I fastened it round her neck, so it couldn't have blown away. I crouch down by the grave and tuck Olive's poppy into one of the metal holes in the vase, but Quetzal wants to know where her necklace has gone. I hear her voice, over and over again, asking me.

Someone took it, I say. *You remember how other people take things. But I brought you a flower instead. See it? It's a poppy.*

Poppies are white, she says in my voice. *Red poppies are for dead people.*

I look at her, straight in her white eyes. Colourless eyes, the way I always liked them, soft under the veil, eyes that don't watch me the way Philip's do. Today it's different, today I need her eyes to see me, to recognize who I am. But they can't. They're just the outside shapes of eyes, white almond shapes without the irises, the round centres that do the seeing.

No, I say. *Red is for the living.*

The white eyes don't blink, don't move at all. She doesn't understand. Very slowly, I get up, my knees shaking like the bones in them were starting to dissolve. Water from the wet grass streams down my legs. The feeling of it makes me shut my eyes, look at what I see inside my eyelids.

What I want to see is how she was, I want to see her running down the pier the way she used to with a half crown in her hand, ready to buy some of those small rubber balls with swirls of colours on them like plasticine. I want to see her bouncing them up against the side wall of the pier theatre, hear the thump as they hit the boards, and her laughing and calling to me to come and watch. I screw my eyes up tighter and tighter and the memory won't come. I've been on the bus, I want to say to Alex, but it isn't working. There's something wrong with the memory.

And what I see instead is colour. I see red, bright cadmium red running down my pale skin like it was on canvas. I'm afraid to open my eyes and look down and find the water's clear. Or if not clear, dirty brown from the grass.

No, I say again. *White is for dead, clear is for dead. Red is the way it used to be.*

I feel a sob coming, dry, like a cough. She doesn't answer, she doesn't argue with me. I open my eyes and look at the folds of her veil, hard and cold and white.

He's gone, I say. *He's gone and he didn't even remember your birthday.*

A thin gust of wind knocks against me, swishes like a soft blow to my face.

Which birthday is it? she says. *How old am I?*

She's breathing the questions at me, trying to make me answer, and I don't. Instead I hear a silence, not like Philip's silence, a silence like the end of the world.

When did I die? she says.

Another rivulet runs slowly down my leg, like a twitch or a very soft gentle touch. I look down, slowly, slowly. And there's no red in it, no red at all. I feel myself start to cry but there's no sound. There are tears in my head, flooding it. I'm drowning in my own head.

I have to go, I say.

The water keeps running until my shoes are full of it. I bend over the grave and start to pull Olive's flower from the vase. The metal holes have gripped the plastic stem and it doesn't want to come but I get it out in the end. I put it inside my shawl and turn my back on her. I move, staggering down the path towards the gate while she calls after me.

Where are you going?

When I get back to the pub my bedroom door is open. I know it's open before I get there, because as I'm coming up the stairs I see the flood of sunlight blanking out the landing, sunlight streaming through my open door. I slow down and stand out on the landing, in the light, looking in at my door as if the room's already gone from me. There's no one there, of course, it's too early for that, but in the middle of the floor, on top of my pale green rug, are some things that weren't there before: a huge tin of paint with dry streams of magnolia running down its sides, and a rectangular tub of plaster. Beside these things are some tools: paint rollers, a large brush with splayed bristles, a diamond-shaped trowel.

Nothing else. I go back out onto the landing but nothing has changed there. The wallpaper is stuck fast to the walls, the greasy phone still hanging at the other end of the landing. It's just inside, in my room. It's a warning, a joke, it's Ralph playing games with me again. If I shut my eyes the things will disappear, or maybe the room will disappear, I can't tell which. I get onto the bed and pull the quilt around me and hold Olive's poppy between my hands. The plastic stamens are hard and spiky but the petals are warm and waxy, they're attached to a ring that lets you move them round on the stem, like the sails on a child's windmill. There are windmills on lots of the graves in the churchyard but I wouldn't have one, in case it blew away.

I lie with my eyes shut. I imagine that I'm Quetzal, cold and white and hardening into gravestone. And then, maybe because of the poppy spiking my hands, maybe because of the windmill, I start to think about church, and Auntie Aileen, and years ago. Not Philip, not ever, not once, not till much later.

And that night the Brylcreem man is back at the hotel window. In fact he arrives early, before I've even tried to sleep. He doesn't sit down to write but comes and stands at the window, with his face in the shadow and the pipe-smoke seeping like steam from the top of his head. He leans his arms on the sash and peers across at me. I can hear him calling my name, calling for an answer.

My mouth opens and closes but no sound comes out of it. I can open my window but it won't make any difference. I hear the Brylcreem man calling *Megan, Megan*, over and over again. And then the words change. He's gesturing with his hands, turning them like he's twisting something, like he's turning a doorknob. I shake my head and then I turn round and see my door still standing open, and now it's dark inside with the landing light spilling in. And finally I work out what it is he's saying.

Shut the door, Megan. Shut the door and tell me all about it.

So I do.

PART II

8.

The train idles for a few minutes and then pulls out of the station the way it came in with that smooth silent way that trains have. Lynn was the only passenger to get off, the only one left on the platform, standing behind her barricade of Mulberry suitcase and Italian leather shoulder bag. Her feet in their new black courts are stuck fast to the concrete; if she looks down she won't see a pair of highly polished shoes but a grazed and bleeding knee, a ladder in her tights moving slowly down her leg from the knee to a twisted ankle.

She fell and grazed her knee alighting from the train. As they slipped into the station she had the window open and her hand ready on the door handle watching the ground as the crumble and stretch of gravel became a slope and then a flat expanse of matt grey concrete. The train jolted and squeaked gently as it came to a halt and she was out of the door, left foot first; only the heel of her right shoe caught on the bottom step and she pitched forward onto the platform, her handbag flung out in front of her, the suitcase half in, half out of the train. Her knee struck first, as a child's would. The impact was like a reflex hammer, aimed at her when she wasn't looking.

It hurts, but she is silent. In the place she has come to, its station so appositely at the end of the line, she cannot risk tears. From here on she will need her feet.

She's dragged herself upright. As she tried to take possession of the right shoe again it slopped against her foot, felt too big, as if she was a child shuffling in her mother's shoes, her trailing skirt, the rattling chain of her

57

long string of false pearls. While the passengers watched from the train, she darted around the platform after her keys, her compact, her tissues and her bunch of lipsticks which spewed out onto the concrete, rolling and blowing with the rubbish; and all this time the carriages slipped by slowly, face after face looking out of the window at her with a kind of incurious interest. *Soundproof glass*, she said to herself, bending once more to retrieve a pack of antiseptic wipes. And, because the soundproofing presumably worked two ways, *Are you all right? Let me help you.*

Don't cry.

Nobody hears her, nobody comforts her. Her bag is back on her right shoulder, the case behind her at her feet. Her gaze stays level with the framed glazed faces, lets each one go without a flicker of expression. As the last carriage passes her the swirling eddy of air behind the train whips her hair up and she has an urge to run, a sudden fear of being left behind, as if the station is an illusion, only visible while the train is stopped there. The panic rises up her body like rewound rain.

Too much Twilight Zone, dumb-ass.

She breathes hard and bends down to get her handbag onto her shoulder. As she bends her skirt tightens across her hips. *Dumb ass, nice ass. Go to hell*, she says, and when she straightens he's gone again but the station is still there. Signboard, benches, list of departures. No toilets, no staff, nobody to carry her suitcases. More Twilight Zone than station, actually. The railway station in the back of her mind has lozenge-shaped signboards with white lettering on a maroon ground, a cafe serving thick black tea and hard white sandwiches stacked like unread books in a perspex display case. It has a station-master's office. The trains have a beginning and an end: at the front the engine with its round sweating face, at the back a brown guard's van like a timber shack, with a kind of veranda at either end. Whenever the train stops the guard gets out with his flag and his black cap with its glossy peak and shouts out the name of the station. She has an awe of the guard, straight and dignified, striding up and down the platform, seeing people on and off the train. Only when he's satisfied the right people are on board can the train depart. When they did RE at school, her first and abiding image of God was of the guard on a train.

There is no guard here, ghostly or otherwise. The platform is deserted; the silence drops in folds like fog behind the departing train. All the windows in the line of sandy brick station buildings are dark; grubby mullions and panes of old spider-webbed glass with no light behind them. Two doors, recently painted sky-blue, firmly padlocked. A lone seagull hops along the line below her, picking bits of somebody's sandwich from between the sleepers. It looks at her, seagull-fashion, with angry, insolent eyes. As she walks slowly down the platform she reads the signs: Private, Watch for Trains, Nearest Toilets in Town. At the far end of the platform, black letters on a white board: Way Out.

Exit, she thinks from habit. The Latinate word, the sharp-edged word, the up-to-date word. One word instead of two. Exits from stuffy theatres, from sports arenas crammed with noise, from examination halls, shuffling closer to the sign in a queue of people. Exits spot lit like paintings in a gallery, hanging over doors in the dark; italic letters on the page of a play-text. *Exit*: and the characters are gone, slipped through an invisible door, leaving their speeches pinned to the page.

Not so Way Out. Two words, a collocation of words chained by use; but with a space between them. Plain

Germanic words, literal, concrete, packed with metaphorical potential. The way out of a fog, a maze, a life, a marriage. Good and bad, depending on where you stand. You might be standing on a cliff top, leaning into the vertical below, taking a jump from the end of land into the sky and pitching down onto the bird-shit splattered rocks and mussel-beds, arms flailing like one of those POWs in The Great Escape. Or standing, as she is right now, at the entrance to this empty cockleshell of a station, before rusted wrought-iron gates topped with Victorian scrollwork. Open gates, dragged backward what looks like years ago to their fullest extent, along a crescent of metal in the ground, a solid track of movement, meaningful as the Greenwich meridian.

Way Out. We choose our words carefully, year 1.

There are three shallow steps downward from the station entrance. She hops herself down to the pavement, because of the stiffness of her knee. For a moment, as both of her feet leave the ground, she feels as if she's flying.

60

9.

Begin at the beginning, says the Brylcreem man, and lights up his pipe again.

But I don't know where the beginning is. I know it's in a place the other side of the headland, the side that isn't real seaside, a place I don't go back to. I was young, I say to him, making the shapes of the words with my mouth so he can see them properly, very young.

He rests his arms on the sash again. The five o'clock car comes up the road and there's a beam of headlamp flashlighting his face. For a moment I see his eyes, looking over me, over the roof of the pub into the darkness outside, into the lonely part of the night. And suddenly I think he can't see me any more. I stretch up, press right into the glass.

I can begin somewhere else, I say. Only I don't know where.

Put your hand out, he says.

I don't know which hand he means, so I put both of them out, straight out from my sides. My left hand goes into nothing, reaches into the cold sponge of darkness until the fingers tingle. My right hand hits the shelves at the side of the room. I sway and fall against them and my hand hits something with sharp edges and smooth sides. Something red.

It's my windmill, the one Auntie Aileen bought me. I take it out, and hold it up. I can't tell if he nods or not.

Windmills are all plastic nowadays, but mine has sails of shiny scarlet attached to a wooden stick. The sails still go round, a bit stiff but they're OK. She bought it for me as a surprise, gave it to me when I'd nearly finished my sandcastle on the beach in the South Bay. I didn't make sandcastles like other children, I built the sides up by scooping sand up into a mound with my hands, I never used a bucket and spade. My castles looked like hills more than towers and turrets, Uncle Simon said. He'd bring me a handful of little pebbles and I'd build a cairn with them on top of my hill and Uncle Simon would laugh. It was Auntie Aileen who thought of the windmill, though. The stick was long enough to go right through the castle to the beach underneath, down to the base of the mound until just the sails showed at the top. But when the wind caught them and they went round with a flapping sound I liked it. If the wind was really strong the sails spun so fast their edges disappeared in a blur and the windmill looked like a ball.

I wouldn't try to spin them now, they might break. But I'm going to keep the windmill all the same.

When I came to live at the seaside Auntie Aileen would sometimes talk to me about my mum and dad. I never asked about them, I knew they both died in hospital when I was making Christmas paper chains, the ones where you lick the end of the paper to make the next link in the chain, and I didn't want to know any more. I could just about remember holidays with my mum playing with me and my dad sitting in a deckchair reading the paper, but as time went by and Auntie Aileen played with me whenever I wanted her it didn't seem to matter. She was a beautiful lady with jet-black hair fluffed out round her head and a soft voice. She wore yellow a lot, and make-up all the time, which she put on at a big dressing-table with a mirror arched like a church window. All the towels in our house were soft and all the baths had to be bubble baths and she'd buy those strawberry and banana ice-cream suckers and say, Who wants the pink one? And I always did. When they talked to us about growing up at school and handed out leaflets with diagrams of your insides in them it sounded frightening and painful, but when I got home and looked at Auntie Aileen, I decided growing up was just becoming more like her.

The only problem she had was Uncle Simon.

I think I had a crush on him. He wasn't good-looking, not in the drop-dead gorgeous way Philip's good-looking, but I always felt happy when he was there. He'd tickle me and pretend to steal my trike and then get his knees stuck under the handlebars and he'd pull faces at the dinner-table and make us laugh. And in the evenings when they had guests and I'd gone to bed I'd hear the laughing and want to join in, so I'd put my pink chiffon housecoat on and go down stairs and look round the door and wait for Uncle Simon to do his astonished face with his hands against his cheeks and his mouth wide open.

I stopped going downstairs after Nicola came.

Nicola worked with Uncle Simon. She wore a black suit and she was middle management, and although I was too young to know how unusual that was in those days I could appreciate the suit. It was made to measure and fitted her like a skin; not like the thick tweedy suits female teachers wore but something more foreign. Italian, Auntie Aileen said when I asked her. And somehow Nicola was a different kind of woman: less an old film star from the black and white movies Auntie Aileen watched on TV, more modern sci-fi, more Alexandra Bastedo, more Emma Peel. She was clever, and Uncle Simon liked that, she could stop him in his tracks when he was joking the way we never could. When she came to dinner there were no more pulled faces, no more monsters made out of napkins and spilt jelly. There were jokes that were all words and no actions, jokes that I could feel but didn't understand.

63

Nicola's jokes weren't for children, but they prodded at me somehow, bruised my insides. And not just me, but Auntie Aileen too: me for being too young for dinner-parties, Auntie Aileen for not knowing all the capital cities of Europe, or understanding TW3. Everyone still laughed, though, even me. But it was a harder kind of laughter, like clapping your hands, like standing up for the Queen. Something you do because other people are doing it too.

'Let's get to bed,' Auntie Aileen would say when the laughter stopped. 'Let's get you all tucked up nice and warm.'

'Goodnight, then, Megan,' Nicola would say, holding up her glass to be filled again.

On those nights I didn't go to Uncle Simon for my kiss.

Nicola came with us to the beach just once, but she didn't play. She smoked and sat in a deckchair next to Uncle Simon while Auntie Aileen and I wrote our names in the wet sand and watched the tide blurring them. Uncle Simon waved at us now and then, but he didn't join in. I read in one of Auntie Aileen's magazines that people who are having an affair get younger and glow before your eyes, but Uncle Simon got older and more distant, too old for games, too grown-up to make faces at the table. After a while too Nicola stopped coming to tea and he went out more and more and came back smelling of drink. I'd lie in bed crying under the eiderdown and hear them downstairs not arguing, precisely, because there was just Uncle Simon's voice shouting and using rude words, words I'd only heard before from boys who were always getting the cane. But I couldn't hear Auntie Aileen talking at all. There was just a low murmur, like the sound you hear if the radio's on very quiet. Like murmuring the responses in church. A soft sound without any real words in it. Only I could hear that Auntie Aileen was losing. She was losing because she didn't have the right words, the strong words.

What was strange was that Uncle Simon didn't move out. He mooched around the house for a while, reading parts of books that Nicola had told him to buy, and he changed the daily paper from the Express to the Guardian, but she got bored with him in the end, the same way she'd made him get bored with us. Deep down he'd been happier going with me to the pictures for Saturday morning cartoons than he was seeing Fellini at the Art House cinema. But he wasn't ever the same afterwards, because he'd been taken in. Now when I took him my Maths homework he'd look bashful and shake his head and say

'All those x's and y's again. They're getting too hard for me, Megan.'

Most of all I remember how it affected Auntie Aileen, how she didn't fight but sort of gathered her softness back into herself, how her voice got quieter and quieter until even I could hardly make out what she was saying. She wasn't clever, but she seemed to know what was coming, that soon you wouldn't be able to be a woman without shouting and using your fists, that softness and gentleness were going out of fashion and they weren't ever coming back. She'd hold my hand ever so kindly and we'd understand each other, that we'd hang on to that part of ourselves no matter what happened, we could look at one another like looking in a misty mirror and know we were still there.

But as I got older I knew she was looking at me less and less. She got to be like an old person, she'd rather sit and embroider cushion covers than go out for the day, she stopped putting her lipstick on and dyeing her hair. And somewhere she stopped being my Auntie Aileen, she left herself behind like an old coat on the bus and she never went back for it. It got so I didn't feel I belonged with either of them any more, so in spite of Nicola I started working hard at school, because when I did my homework I got a smile, and the teacher would say my name, say it as if I meant something. And slowly I worked my way up Good to Very Good and sometimes Excellent, words even Uncle Simon would still take notice of, and pat me on the head and talk about going to college. Auntie Aileen would be listening to the Archers, or just napping in her chair. And what was most awful was that for a long time I thought it was her let me down, not Uncle Simon. She hadn't stood firm, she hadn't stood in solidarity with me. Only I'd missed the point, but I didn't see that until years afterwards.

And for a long while I had this dream about Auntie Aileen, or my mum, I was never sure which of them it was. We were standing in the middle of a road with a lorry careering down the hill coming towards us, and Auntie Aileen's arms were round me, but she was behind me, and I knew the lorry would hit me first. I'd wake up gasping, not clever, not excellent. Those words were just covers I pulled over myself. And there wasn't any warmth in them.

But I was at college by then. And at college I met Philip.

10.

There is a tramp outside the station. A rather scrawny, ill-fed, scrag-end-of-neck kind of specimen, sitting cross-legged on the pavement wearing loud brown and white check trousers, a dirty cream polo-neck and a white sunhat. He is scruffy but strangely well-composed, as dapper as the corpse of an elderly golfer drying in the sun. Upturned in front of him on the pavement is a much better hat than the one he's wearing, a velvet one with a wide brim containing a few two pence pieces. The tramp doesn't hassle her or snarl Have a Nice Day behind her back with traditional beggar's sarcasm, so a couple of yards past him she stops, puts down her suitcase and hunts in her bag for some change. Her purse contains nothing except a twenty pound note and a two pound piece, so she fishes out the gold and silver coin, drops it in the hat, nods and glances briefly at him. He has very blue eyes. Dark blue, but blue all the same, peeking sharply up at her from under the white sunhat brim like the stalky eyes of crabs in a rock-pool. He says something, but his voice is so hoarse the words are unclear. The quality of the voice is that of sandpaper, but old, worn-out sandpaper. As he makes the effort to speak his throat stands to attention like a chicken's, taut under the bandage of the stained roll of his polo-neck jumper. There's something familiar about the sound he makes, something Lynn can't quite place. She turns her face to the town, picks up her luggage and sets off again.

After a minute she looks back. The tramp has left his pitch and is trotting along the pavement at some distance behind her, also in the direction of the town. His walk is pigeon-toed, not quite a jog but a bumpy, rolling gait, reminiscent of a speed-walker at the Olympics. Lynn faces forward and quickens her pace a little, until she's slightly out of breath. Her knee begins to throb with the pounding, her chest tightens with annoyance. There were no beggars here before she left. Beggars are a contemporary phenomenon, trailing cardboard boxes, cans of Stella and dark rain-washed inner-city streets in their wake; this, on the contrary, is an old-fashioned seaside resort with its arrested context of buckets and spades and deckchairs and Punch and Judy on their red and white miniature stage, their rigid papier-maché faces clearly resolved in the brilliant turquoise sea-reflected daylight.

Although at this end of the town some of the shops are boarded up, and many of the remaining shop-fronts have a slightly shabby 60s air. From a hairdresser's window a row of polystyrene heads look out at the street with blank white eyes, chiffon scarves knotted round their necks, butter-coloured backcombed wigs pulled down low over their bald white foreheads. *Closed until*, the notice says on the door, with a little plastic clock set to half past nine beneath it. Lynn goes up to the door and peers past the clock into the dim interior of the salon. Black PVC chairs and archaic helmet hairdryers. She hasn't sat underneath one of those since she was a bridesmaid in her teens, with her burning head held in a vice of tightly wound rollers with their sea-urchin spines, her body swathed in a black nylon shroud, her hand clamped sweatily around the joystick of the heating control, trying to turn the dial to Low without anyone noticing. The stylist had combed her out into a misty tower of hair, losing her fine plucked eyebrows under a curve of hefty fringe. And when the wedding was over and the hairpins finally pulled out she took to bed with her a head of curls that bounced like party streamers and smelled of Elnett.

Only by the morning her hair was, as her mother would have said, straight as tapwater.

She takes a step backward. *Monique*, the signboard says in slightly shaky black italic on a yellow ground. Birkenhead French, she thinks to herself with a tight smile, circa 1965. Nowadays even hairdressers' names are postmodern and ironic: *Streaks Ahead, Shampers, Crowning Glory.*

Curl Up and Dye.

The tramp is still coming. She can hear him wheezing, but he doesn't quit. Further up the road, the sun glints on the aluminium of the (up to date) outside tables and chairs of a cafe. Lynn power-walks the remaining few yards and makes for the open door. Inside the cafe, the furniture is of an earlier vintage; honey pine tables draped with chequered tablecloths, dark pine match-boarded walls. There are even waitresses. She grounds her suitcase, takes the table furthest from the window and a chair with its back to the wall, and orders a cappuccino.

The calm, civilized smell of the coffee revives her. She's spooning the froth into a creamy swirl when the tramp comes in and flops himself down at a table opposite hers.

She begins to rise, and stops herself. It can only be a matter of moments before he's ejected. He nods at her, takes off his sunhat and drops it over the cruet in the centre of the table. His uncovered hair is wispy, longish, apparently clean; he licks a finger and smarms a few strands across the bald patch that tops his head, tonsure-fashion. The waitress advances, pen and pad in hand and he croaks a few words at her, pointing to something on the menu.

The girl bends, alarmingly close, to see what he's looking at. She's student age, her dark hair scraped severely back from a face lanced with a number of piercings: left nostril, right eyebrow, lower lip. And a row of silver hoops like curtain-rings down the length of both earlobes. On her evenings off, the odds are she works the fairground, or the promenade, or fraternizes with the night-fishermen who line the pier. Another dweller in the hinterland, closer to the tramp than the coffee-drinkers. She scribbles, disappears into the kitchen to fill whatever order he has given. Lynn swiftly scans the menu, discovers that the place is licensed. *A vat of house red*, she thinks. *Pernod and cider. Ten fingers of Johnnie Walker.* And suddenly she finds herself turning to Phil to share the joke, her memory kicking up at her like a reflex.

But the tramp has ordered ice cream. A tall Knickerbocker-Glory glass crammed with pink and white scoops of it, a fan-shaped wafer on the top. He falls on it like a child, removing the wafer and laying it on his hat, digging down through the cold globes of vanilla and raspberry with his long-handled spoon. With every mouthful he parts his lips and pants once or twice, showing a small pinkish mass melting gently on his protruding tongue. The froth dries in the bottom of Lynn's cappuccino, her hands tighten around the cup. She's quiet and discreet in her shadow, but the sharp blue crab-eyes are aware of her. The tramp catches the corner of her glance and smiles, the three teeth in his upper jaw glistening with their ice-cream coating. One skinny hand reaches out toward the hat; he picks up the wafer, and holds it out to her. Lynn looks at her coffee, stirs the crusty froth in the bottom of her cup; he gets up, still holding out the wafer.

It's time to leave, to prove her disappearing woman trick still works. Her chair-back scrapes a pale line on the varnished dado behind her. Even to get to the till she'll have to pass him. The waitress is leaning on the counter, arms folded, examining her black lacquered nails. Lynn is on her feet, attempting a swerve around the tramp's arm, her twenty-pound note crumpled in her fist. As she pays the bill and drops her change, willy-nilly, into the makeup pocket of her handbag, she can feel the bony insolence of down-and-out flesh pressing hers, the dirty pungent fabric of down-and-out sweater brushing her wrist. The wafer fan is so close to her face she can smell it.

'Yours,' the tramp croaks at the back of her head. 'Madame Pompadour.'

Over the scalloped edge of the fan Lynn can see the bus stop outside the cafe and a maroon and white bus standing at the stop, its engine idling. She pushes against the tramp's arm and he falls back into his seat, arms and legs flailing, like a shot marshal in a western. Somebody laughs, but she doesn't wait to find out who it is. She drags herself and her luggage out of the cafe, across the pavement and up the three steps of the bus, gasping and struggling with her suitcase like an old woman with a shopping trolley. Pasted to the driver's door is a list of fares: 50p, 70p, 90p. She empties her fist of currency and collapses onto a seat.

The bus starts up. She's at the roadside window, her head turned firmly to the glass, her right cheek against the coolness of it. The bus smells, surprisingly, of leather, but there's the scent of vanilla on her fingers, vanilla from the ice-cream she didn't taste, from the wafer she knocked, presumably, into a thousand honey-coloured crumbs. Superior wafers, sweet and melting and layered like mica, wholly unlike the mean oblong slabs of cardboard that came with an ice-cream brick. As a child she had hoarded the boxes, distinctive fan-shaped boxes with an illustration of La Pompadour in her ribboned straw hat and her eighteenth-century buckled shoes, her stiff swagged shepherdess skirt billowing around her. A doomed pink and white doll on a bright turquoise background, the same turquoise as the stiff taffeta bridesmaid's dress that hung for months on the back of her bedroom door, holding its shape stubbornly, month after weary month, dust collecting on the polythene cover dropped over the shoulders.

She was never asked to be a bridesmaid again, and couldn't have worn the same dress if she had been. But by the time her mother was prepared to consider the idea of selling it plump, waisted taffeta had gone out of fashion, and Empire line was in.

She looks down, to stop herself from looking back. Along with the bus ticket in her hand there's the bill from the cafe. Smoothing it out, she realizes that she has paid for the ice cream.

11.

I'm tired out with so much remembering, so I sleep. Sometime during the night I wake up, and see Alex sitting in the chair beside my bed. He's got himself some new winter clothes, black fleecy tracksuit bottoms and a thick grey cardigan that loses his arms and hands as well inside it, so just his cigarette points out of the cuff like the stub of an amputated finger. He's sitting in my old child's chair with its brown studded back and curved wooden arms, the one I sat in for years in between Uncle Simon and Auntie Aileen, watching Fireball XL5 on the television and having my Hovis and Marmite supper. The chair's so low Alex can't really sit in it properly, he stretches his legs out as if he was lying on the floor, his head sinks into his neck between his hunched shoulders. He looks like the Incredible Shrinking Man, not fitting into anything, getting smaller and smaller before he slips through a crack in the floorboards.

I like having him there, so I turn myself onto my side where I can see him as I fall asleep.

'Not to worry, Megan,' he mumbles into his cardigan. 'Not to worry, the cavalry's coming.'

But I'm drifting off, drifting into dreams with Alex going clop, clop into his turned-up collar.

When the light starts to poke through the curtains the chair's empty. There's just the Brylcreem man across the street, his pipe out, his head down over his arms. *Where's Alex,* I want to say, *what have you done with Alex?* But I don't. Instead I roll over, get out of bed and start to get dressed. I move very quietly, making myself busy. Through the eyes at the back of my head I see the Brylcreem man look up. I don't know if it's the movement that wakes him, or the sound of my thoughts, but I know he hears me thinking, hears me so I feel as if I might never have to talk again. The daylight grows and grows and gleams on the slick of hair waving across his forehead. There's a frozen feel to him, a hardness that makes me think of Philip. Philip not as he was, but as he became, cooling through the years.

That's right, he says. *You were going to tell me about Philip.*

He lights his pipe again. This time the glow is orange.

What are you doing? he says.

I don't know why he needs to ask. I'm painting, the brush thick and dripping in my hand, my arm moving back and forth across the door. I paint with broad strokes from side to side, pushing the bristles into the mouldings around the door, spattering the wall beyond the frame with wet dark stars. There's an abstract look to the spattering that I like. It's something that might have got me through college, kept me from falling through the floor of my life when I'd barely started living it. Something I'm finding too late.

What I used to do, I say. *What I was doing before Philip came along, what I was doing when he came along.*

And the stars swell with paint, an instant before they start to run down the walls.

The course was called Diploma in Art and Design. I was always more Art than Design, because nothing I painted was ever of any use to anyone, and that made it Art, or so Nigel used to say. I was terrified of most of the students but Nigel cheered me up. He'd get old fridges and cookers from the council and take the doors off, then he'd paint the insides orange and go and sit in them, all tucked up with his knees against his chin like a baby. He was a kind of early punk with a torn school blazer and spiky yellow hair, and the tutors loved him, they'd go and photograph him squatting in his cookers and if they asked he'd refuse to say what the art meant, but each piece had a price-tag attached to it with the title, only the titles were just things like Hotpoint, or Indesit, or Belling. Nigel could get away with things in a way I never could with my watercolour pictures of knights and ladies and my misty landscapes with hills and churches and towers. Whatever I did, everything turned out looking as if Auntie Aileen had painted it, it was too soft, none of my colours were loud enough, none of the lines I drew held together; they trailed off into nothing, there were gaps in them, like aeroplane smoke-trails broken up by the wind.

But I wanted to do well. Uncle Simon liked me being at college, he'd ask me how it was going and he'd look at my pictures, even though he didn't know what to say about them. One he seemed to like especially, it had a delicate spider's web weighed down with raindrops, and the threads of the web stretched across the whole picture; through them you could see a frog sitting on a riverbank and a blue river beyond. I was pleased with the web, the lines were fragile but there weren't any gaps in them, and Nigel said the raindrops looked as if they'd fall off if he touched them; but what Uncle Simon liked was the frog. He even made a very small croaking sound in his throat like he'd have done when I was a child and I smiled, I remembered. But the memory hurt, deep down in my stomach.

Once Nicola was long gone Uncle Simon got much nicer again, and if he couldn't manage to laugh at cartoons any more he was sort of humbler. He still drank whisky, but at home, from a Waterford glass in front of the telly, and I hadn't heard him shout at Auntie Aileen for a long time.

About ten o'clock he'd disappear into his study and whenever I brought some paintings home he'd ask for one to pin up on the study wall, never a knights-and-ladies picture but a landscape. There was a group of about ten, I'd painted the same picture over and over again because I didn't know quite what it was. The pictures were of a rounded hill and a purple sky with shaky clouds, and a building on top of the hill, maybe a church, a castle, or just a few pointed rocks. And a winding path leading up to the building. All of them, Uncle Simon said when I showed him my folder, but he didn't ask what they were supposed to be. The only picture he ever mentioned was the spider's web one, the first time I was old enough to go out to the college bar and I came into his study in my thigh-length grey suede boots with glitter on my hair, and he looked at the frog very solemnly and stretched his lips out and kind of flexed them a couple of times, like he was trying to find an old joke in the dark.

'Remember, Megan,' he said, 'They don't become princes. They're just frogs.'

The tutors were frogs, and they were the reason I wanted to go to the bar. Or not frogs at all, something more essentially human, more like Nicola. Not liking my pictures wasn't enough for the tutors; they needed to have something to use their words on, not just sharp cruel words but gentler words like soft, and girlish, and fragile, that they pulled and twisted until they weren't gentle any more. The tutors hunted in pairs: one of them would flip through the stuff in my portfolio and the other would stand with arms folded, choosing the words like sweets, chewing them like gum till they were grey and tasteless. Nigel did his best for me, he hung around behind them and told them they were mother-fixated middle-aged arseholes with crap taste in Double-Two shirts and took me off to the bar. And after the first gin it seemed okay again. When I drank I sort of grew another skin, one the words didn't get through.

The college bar was like all other college bars in the seventies. All the seats and tables were too low and made of matt-black painted pinewood, and the glasses and slops just piled up at lunchtime until the mass exodus at two o'clock. The only time it ever looked okay was at night, when you couldn't see very much. You weren't supposed to drink spirits because the company had been involved with thalidomide, so I'd usually give my money to whichever guy was going to the bar and ask if he'd get my gin. One night a crowd of students from Performing Arts were around the table with the Art and Design crowd and they were arguing about the poor people with thalidomide, how they couldn't get any money from Distillers and it was all going through the courts, and how we all had to take responsibility.

Somebody was in the middle of telling the others about a poster he'd seen of a baby with no arms and legs when Nigel came back from the bar with his Day-glo splashed hands around three pints of Guinness and a gin and orange and plonked them down in the middle of the table. Three hands came out to claim the pints and left the plastic tumbler with the gin and orange on its own. And the student with the poster said:

'Whose is *that*?'

Nobody said anything. I remember I wanted my drink so much, especially the first couple of sips, because I knew how the gin would have risen to the top, how it would be clear and strong with the little piece of ice on the surface and sticky orange at the bottom. And Nigel was tugging at his yellow tufts of hair in the way he always did when he was embarrassed, and muttering something like Cool it, man, only not loud enough. Not loud enough.

Then the table went into shadow and the sparkle went from the surface of the gin. Someone leant over my chair from behind and grabbed the plastic glass by its rim with his fingertips and took the drink away. There was a waft of fresh air with a clean smell to it, a swimming-baths kind of smell, and a violin-bow twang to the voice projecting into the middle of the group.

'Okay, let's change the subject, shall we? Ladies present.'

I turned round. He was holding up the glass to the light, swilling the liquid round. He had a sip, looked at me, handed it over.

'Beats cyanide,' he said.

He was in a t-shirt and loons like we all were, but black as opposed to beige and cream and brown like the rest of us. Although it was hard to pick out colours in the green light from the beer-pumps, his eyes were pale and his hair looked white, in a sort of unkempt pageboy style. But he had a man's face, not a girlish one like so many of the other boys. Intense, but a different intensity to Nigel painting his fridges with his tongue sticking out the side of his mouth. A kind of future-history intense, so his eyes were less like a photograph of whatever had happened in his life, more of whatever was going to happen. I said to Nigel afterwards it was all in the colour, that you can't look blue in the face the way you can brown. The next term Nigel started doing a lot of canvases with blue in them, mostly cerulean, great pools of oil paint pushing out the other colours. I was quite proud, as if I'd done them myself.

Once I'd got my drink, Philip slid into the seat beside me, getting his face in the way of the green light, stretching his left arm along the black pine backrest of the bench. I drank my gin in the shadow he made, watching his right hand perched on the table, the fingers slightly gathered, flexing, waiting to take the glass up for a refill as soon as I was ready.

And as I drank my body went soft and comfortable, bending like a rag doll. It was a feeling I'd never forget, a gratitude I'd never manage to lose. Some people don't like to be thanked, but Philip did, it was a word he never tired of.

About a week after that first night, Philip and I came back from our pub lunch to find that somebody had scrawled over one of the pictures I'd left in the studio. *Armless and legless,* it said in rough black charcoal, the black running into the wet watercolour beneath.

Philip tore the picture to pieces in front of all the other students. And that was an end of it. Nobody defaced my knights and ladies again, nobody even noticed them, much. At assessment time, they'd get covered up with other people's work, turned face down so all you could see of the picture were the coloured blurs, like bruises, where the paint had soaked through to the other side. Nigel said if only I would look closely there was something in the blurs that was interesting, but I didn't look, I wouldn't look.

Painting wasn't something I did much of, anyway, after that night. It got to feel like something I'd put behind me, or off to one side. I spent a lot of time looking in mirrors, always with my radio on, planning. I had my hair done strawberry blonde, which was really a sort of toffee colour and not too close to Philip's platinum. In the evenings I'd tie a thin cream ribbon round my forehead and bow it over my ear with the ends trailing down, I wore long cheesecloth skirts and gypsy blouses with bell sleeves, I did my eyes with kohl and my cheeks with burgundy blusher and bronze-gold highlighter. Nigel didn't like any of it, he said I'd become Design, and all designers were prostitutes, they'd got USE ME written all the way through them like sticks of rock.

He was right, of course, but I didn't care. He was right as well when he said Philip pulled me along behind him by my cream satin ribbon, that in the right light he could see a string pulled tight between us, fine and almost invisible, like a fishing-line, taut and strong and cruel. But it was when he talked about the colours I paid the most attention. He said that Philip wanted something from me and that the something was yellow. Blue and yellow are primaries and blue needs yellow to make green, and green was what Philip needed. It got so I couldn't go into the college studio without Nigel ranting colour metaphors at me and though I'd sit perched on a stool and listen to him for ages, what happened in the end was that Nigel kept painting and I didn't. And at the time I never bothered because with Philip there was always a diversion, a something else to watch.

The something else that year for drama students was the degree class production of H G Wells' *Things To Come*. It was so good it got a mention in the Guardian and a scout from the BBC came to the last night. Philip was Arden Essenden, one of the new world leaders in the faceless state who gets involved in an affair and is ordered by the ruling council to take his own life. In the very last scene of the play, Philip stood on the stage in his black flying suit in front of a huge blow-up of his own face, with just one white spotlight on him and the cyanide pill held up between his thumb and forefinger and his expression was right, his eyes were right, everything was right. And I looked at him and thought, He'll never come back. Not to that moment in the bar when he rescued me for drinking gin, not to the moment when he changed the subject and took charge of my glass and gave my order, time after time, like it was a line he'd always known by heart.

When the play was over the audience stood up to applaud and Philip came through the closed red curtains and stood with his hands behind him, bowing every so often to acknowledge the cheers. Each time he raised his head I could see him looking out at the audience, peering at the first few rows where the stage lights reached to the faces, and I was waving like mad and blowing kisses. Only by the time I got into the dressing room he was angry, he was dragging dark red greasepaint off his chin and lips and his mouth was white underneath.

'The bastard just left,' he said. 'Just left and never came backstage.'

It was the first time I'd ever heard him swear. I felt as if I should say something, but he was talking into the mirror, digging his hand into the cold cream until it was brown as sand and smearing it on his cheeks, flecks of greasepaint spotting the glass, his stage face melting in the grease. I opened the door and slipped out to see if he was wrong, if the BBC man was really waiting in the corridor, his collar turned up against the draught like a 30s detective, holding out a contract in his hand that would change everything, make Philip's real face the same as his stage one.

But as I opened the door again I heard his voice, swearing, angry, just the same. I don't think he noticed that I'd gone.

Of course Nigel had been there, in the front row, as intrusive as he could get without actually rushing the stage. All he said in the bar after the performance was that Philip had got his green at last.

And his new surname, but Nigel never knew about that. Philip had it changed by deed poll the week after he graduated.

12.

The bus indicates and moves out into the traffic. On the broad main street there's a queue of cars, many of them also indicating, loitering around in the centre of the road, trying to find parking spaces. The bus driver swears at them in some language that is not English, winds in and out, and eventually turns in to the long curve of road that edges the seafront. From the windows of the bus on Lynn's side the town falls away into the concrete of the promenade, the concrete falling away in its turn into the conglomerate of rubble, into pebbles and sand. Mounded at the top of the beach are large grey-blue pebbles, striped pebbles, purple skimmers, tiny white pebbles; all of them being broken down into smaller and smaller chunks on their way down the stone chain, until they're ready to be folded into the froth of an ebb wave like egg-whites vanishing into cake mixture. By the time the sea has done with them, the stones are washed smooth of all traces of building; they're rounded, mobile again, ready to move out from land, to be sucked away into the blue, into the vague distant wash of colour out to sea which is where the horizon should be.

Lynn is not sitting where she normally sits on a bus. Usually she'd take a seat far enough back from the driver as to make it unlikely that anyone would join her, far enough back not to feel pressured into giving up her seat for young girls with staring pastry-faced babies or old people with walking sticks and tough tanned skin. But she was rushed, and she's at the front, immediately behind the driver, with a wide view out to her right but nothing in front of her but a perspex partition and a black blind pulled down beyond it to screen the driver. She stares at the blind, envying the man's closed back, the clear demarcation of his visible and invisible halves. At first the seat behind her is empty, but at the pull-in on the promenade several more passengers board the bus, and now there are two old ladies chattering away behind her about holidays and hotels. Their words batter her neck, their heavily ringed hands grip the top rail of the seat in front of them, knuckling her shoulder. The rings catch stray hairs from her ponytail, they tug on the hairs and tighten them like fishing-line: they are as cold as if just reeled in from the deep sump of sea beneath the pier.

The two old ladies have just discovered that they are staying in the same hotel. Their voices surge in excitement, their hands abandon the top rail in order to follow the turn of their grey-mauve heads, to gesture and point toward the rear of the bus.

Esplanade! the voices shriek. *Esplanade!*

Lynn looks up at the soft carpeted ceiling of the bus. Right above her seat is a round red plastic button surrounded by a circle of highly polished chrome.

Press Once, it says on the circle.

She starts to raise her arm, changes her mind. She can see them, these old ladies with their knuckle-duster hands and carborundum voices, meeting unexpectedly on the hotel stairs with the green carpet and white-painted banisters; one is on her way up from the hall with its neo-Georgian reception desk, lit by a modest chandelier suspended from a wavy ceiling rose, a chandelier with one of its glass candles missing; one is on her way down from the dark unlit landing with the green trunk covered in piles of old fashion magazines. Only one of the ladies has a suitcase: the one coming up the stairs. They greet each other, but without gladness, preoccupied by the knowledge that one of them will have to give way, still undecided on who it's going to be.

But it's not them she sees, of course. It's someone else.

The bus gives its passengers a jolt as it rolls out onto the road that goes around the headland. With the mist clinging round the cliffs there isn't much to see, although a vaguely topographical commentary has started to issue from the other side of the black blind. Unlike the undistinguished shale that makes up the rest of the coast, the headland is composed of carboniferous limestone; and this limestone is eroding in the salt air, salt that dissolves bits of the cliffs each year and sends rivers of stones down into the sea. Pale landslips trickle onto the road in small stone floods, slipping their soil and scree through the holes of the metal mesh that is pinned across vast swathes of the cliff side to hold them back. Sometimes after winter storms larger boulders break free, hurtling down from the summit onto the road and into the water, bouncing like medicine balls until they strike sea-level and crack open on the gritty stones that rattle in and out with the tide.

The view out to sea comes and goes. Through one of the occasional holes in the mist something that looks like a red buoy appears, bobbing in the slaty shattered water below them, but as they get closer the buoy turns into a large cotton reel with scarlet tubing for thread. It's hard to know if the reel was lost from land or sea: whether it rolled away unnoticed behind the backs of workmen laying cable somewhere along the coast, or dropped from the deck of a container ship in the swell, splashing into an ice-cream sea and floating jerkily, helplessly, as the rusty overloaded hull shrank in the distance, its white wake broken up by the wind.

The mist drops and the reel disappears. There is a twelfth-century church on the headland, and the bus pulls off the road and stops in a lay-by so that the passengers can get a better look at it, but the mist has reduced the building to a grey triangle on the skyline with a square hole punched in its apex to house a single bell. Around the church the cemetery swells in a green mound. Leaning gravestones protrude from their mossy hill, bristling like a small felled forest with just the stumps of trees left. Nearer the church the stones are grey, but closer to the road they are whiter, more recent and more ornate: marble crosses twisted with white ivy, crosses topped by urns draped with white starched fabric, marble angels with uplifted goose-feather wings. The driver asks, as seems customary, whether anyone wants to get out and look at the church, and Lynn stares flatly out to what's left of the sea view, giving thanks for the weather, while the two old ladies answer for the rest of the bus.

There is no view on the way back to town. The mist turns Scotch and salts the windscreen of the bus with every sweep of the wipers; the rest of the windows sweat and blur with the passengers' breath. The pavement fringing the road runs along beside them with its accompanying wall, rising and falling with the ground like a grey rope warding off a chasm. They pass a single pedestrian walking on the pavement, going in the same direction as the bus: a woman in a white blouse, a long skirt and flip-flops, holding a sopping bunch of flowers wrapped in clotted, multi-coloured paper. It's raining lightly, but this woman is wet enough to have been dipped in the sea, her hair smeared brown and glistening across her head as if she surfaced under a drift of kelp. She doesn't look at the bus as it passes her but strides out, the kelp hair swinging with her gait, water squirting from her sandals at each step.

Lynn turns, to get a better look, but the bus bends round a corner and the woman disappears from sight. Lynn waits for the two old ladies to comment, but they've gone quiet, rustling a bag of sweets and masticating slowly, like cows chewing cud. She has an urge to tell the driver to stop and go back, she wants to turn round and stare one of the carborundum voices into life, to ask them if she was the only passenger to see the woman, but she's left it too late. The black blind gags her own voice like a frosted pastille stuck in her throat.

As they draw into the terminus in town there's just one person waiting. The tramp is standing on the wooden seat beside the bus shelter, holding part of a cardboard box above his head, a piece of cardboard with a word written across it in thick black magic marker, like the signs held out by people waiting for someone at airports.

Esplanade, it says. The two old ladies splutter into life.

13.

Of course, I didn't graduate. I didn't even do much soul-searching, because the way I saw it my life had already gone somewhere else, and I needed to rush off and catch it up. Nobody at college cared much, anyway. I had to go and see the Head of Department in his office, which was white and chocolate brown and leathery, what you'd call nowadays minimalist. The Head of Department was double-barrelled, Leigh-hyphen something, and Scottish, like most of the doctors I'd ever known, and he smelled of leather and pipe tobacco. He flipped through my sketchbooks, which were small, with small pencil drawings in them, unlike the enormous folders and coloured cartridge paper with heavy charcoal scribbles all over it that everyone else had. And he said, I don't remember exactly, but something like, that they did a lot of weeding out in the first year anyway, that it was as well to find out you weren't cut out to be an artist earlier rather than later on.

I don't think I agreed with him, but he didn't ask me to. He didn't ask me anything, just kept flipping through my books and creasing the edges of the pages. And looking at his brown stained thumb. If only he'd looked at me, I've often thought, suggested I reconsider my decision, instead of letting me slide out the door like the Invisible Woman, or under it, I was small enough already to do that. But other people are so busy in their own lives they don't notice they're leaning on yours, looking through you, not talking to you so you can't talk back. Leaving you alone.

Even when I was younger and my bones were more solid I wasn't much good on my own. There's a lot of rubbish talked about doing everything for yourself. Doing everything for yourself makes you weary, it empties you out till you're like a Pyrex dish with all the food scraped away. You become silent, willing somebody to touch your hand, to ask you something, even directions on the street. Silent but with a dark egg of anger inside you. A hard egg, boiled too long until the yolk inside has a hard black line around it. Every day you say nothing, you try to swallow the egg and it won't go down. It sticks in your throat, in the way of the voice. The voice tries to squeeze around the egg and when it comes out it's thin and wispy; and for a while, whenever you try to speak, people turn around and ask you to repeat what you said. And then they don't.

After college I had the egg all the time. The doctor sent me to what you'd call an assertiveness therapist and on Wednesdays I went to a group that met in a ramshackle house in town and sat around in a circle on old furniture and talked about the terrible things people, mostly parents, had done to them. Nobody had ever done anything terrible to me, so I couldn't say much. But I noticed that although a lot of the other people were angry or tearful, they didn't have the egg. Instead they had stories of incest and beating with sticks and belts and fathers climbing into their cots; and when they'd finished telling the stories the rest of us had to applaud, like it was a talent contest. And in a way it was. A shouting competition, voices billowing out and filling the corners of the room, making even the spiders run for cover. The worst story won every time, sucking up the oxygen till I could only breathe in tiny, shallow gasps.

Needless to say I came nowhere. The doctor wrote on my notes - I watched her write it, I can read upside down - that I was a classic victim, but I knew I was just the thinnest seagull. You can see a group of seagulls, any day of the week, a muddle of yellow feet and beaks and grey wings flapping over the prom like windblown garbage, fighting over a single chip paper with a bit of batter in it. It's the seagull with the biggest gape that wins, the one with the shrillest call. Humans are just seagulls when they're hungry. The thin ones are the lonely ones.

When the doctor had finished writing, she asked me what I thought I could do now, in a brisk, pull-yourself-together sort of voice.

I said I could still be a woman.

Philip hadn't abandoned me. If anything, he was around more than ever. He was starting to get acting work, repertory mostly; summer season whodunits, Agatha Christie and so on, but no Shakespeare or Pinter or Stoppard. The third Star Wars film was out, and there was quite a sci-fi revival. The roles Philip was offered didn't usually have many lines but because of the Wells he was quite in demand for a while and, as his agent said, If you already look like someone from another planet, why fight it? Philip played so many silver-suited aliens on TV he started to get on the convention circuit. I went with him once to the Holiday Inn in Manchester, but he didn't warn me about the clothes. I still had my long skirts and gypsy blouses and ribbons and that was past tense, where everything had to be future. The female science fiction fans wore black Lycra bodysuits and tinsel wigs and huge silver armour-plated shoulder pads like American football players and they made for Philip like he was the ball and closed ranks around him.

Philip never saw much harm in them. He shed all the nonsense with the costume when he came off stage, but I didn't, I saw the harm. The convention women were like Nicola, like the airgirl in The Shape of Things to Come. In Wells's book the airgirl commits suicide rather than break up Arden Essenden's marriage, but these women weren't going to crash their bright shiny planes for any man or any woman, for that matter. They were supposed to make you feel that all the old barriers were down, that a new woman could do anything, be anything, even Prime Minister, but what they made me feel was frightened, uneasy, like they were a new gender altogether, grown in a test tube from 60s ideas, but without any of the 60s grace; and my gender, mine and Auntie Aileen's, was slowly dying out. It was all in the shoulders, in those thick white foam pads you had to sew into every blouse and sweater you possessed, that pushed their outline through the fabric, shadowing your breastbone like an X-ray of your lung. They weren't designed for kindness or understanding but for barging, for pushing the old gender off the pavement, into the traffic. Knowing we were like hedgehogs, like rabbits, slow, frantic, frozen in the lights, unable to adapt. Dinosaurs.

I was a dinosaur. That's why Sapphire suited me so well.

We were very proud of the shop-front at Sapphire. The signboard was a shiny deep blue, as glossy as three coats of Revlon nail polish, and it had the name picked out in white Roman lettering. The clothes in the window display always made us look like a wedding outfitter's; lemon or pale pink dresses and suede sandals and glittery little handbags for the women, smart three-piece suits in cream corduroy or pinstripe for the men. And hats, Betty loved to display hats, straw, velvet, felt, flowers or no flowers, the bigger the better. She insisted on dressing the models in the window herself; she wouldn't let us call them dummies. The dummies were the shoppers, the people who crossed the threshold without realizing we were actually an agency, one of those places where people take their old clothes to resell for money. Except the clothes had to be smart and freshly laundered and not old at all, as Betty would explain to anyone assuming we were some kind of charity shop.

She had her standards, and her standards were very high. She would put on her glasses with their gold chain hanging from her temples and hold up the Laura Ashley dresses to the light - we got a lot of Laura Ashleys in those days - and check the flounces for fraying and the collars and sleeves for grease and stains. Then she'd untie the belts and sashes and try the zips and say, eventually, always the same thing,

'How much were you thinking of for this, dear?'

There were two kinds of shoppers. The kind who came in once, accidentally, and never again, and the kind who ceased to be dummies, and became customers; wedding guests, Betty called them. If they were selling, she never went above her price for a garment, but once they were in they were likely to buy, not because they needed clothes, but because they wanted a little piece of Sapphire. We were a second-hand version of the old Biba, a kind of sparkling murky cave full of wonderful useless things, but things you had to have, the way you had to buy something from Biba once you were inside, even if it was just a black lipstick or a purple feather. Only Sapphire was light colours, not dark, a kind of Biba at the seaside with the prices marked down accordingly; the feather boas were white or pink, and the chiffon and viscose scarves were suspended from the ceiling like a washed-out rainbow on a sort of clothes-dryer, hanging just low enough to brush people's foreheads and make them look up. We never had those curvy Biba hatstands, Betty thought they were unstable and likely to get us into trouble with the feet of the older customers. Instead the hats were piled on the glass top of a white melamine dressing table with a triptych mirror edged in gold scrollwork, the sort of dressing table that was very smart in the mid-60s. There was a notice in front of the mirror, asking customers to sit down at the dressing-table if they wanted to try any of the hats. Betty said it deterred the wrong sort of customer, and most of the time she was right.

By and large the new gender left us alone. It would be years before retro became fashionable; in those days long dresses and feather boas were just nostalgic or embarrassing. I expected to feel safe again, but I didn't. Somewhere between Nicola and the Scottish professor and the black lycra women I'd begun to realize that I didn't matter. Not in the scheme of things, whatever the scheme of things was. Periodically my life dropped from beneath my feet like a stand collapsing at a football match and I had to follow it down, arms flailing, waiting for someone to spot me in the wreckage the way Philip had spotted me. Sapphire wasn't exactly wreckage, but it was lower than the place I'd started from, somewhere I knew I'd fallen into from a height. I could feel invisible purple bruises on my hips where I'd hit the ground.

The clothes helped. One of my jobs was to sort them into size and type - summer jackets, long or short skirts, evening dresses or whatever, and keep the rails tidy. I got so I could tell at a glance what would fit me. Once people knew about us we got a lot of 70s designer clothes, Mary Quant and Ralph Lauren and I had my own Biba original, a long cream sheath dress with a scooped-out back and a sort of train. The fabric had a soft shine on it like the inside of an oyster, and fine, elasticated pleating, which opened up and clung to you when you put the dress on; and when you took it off the pleats folded, and scrunched down almost to nothing, like the sticks of a fan. The train had been torn where somebody had stepped on it, and with all the pleats it wasn't easy to mend. You could still make out a jagged tear, like a crack in a wall which moved, opened or closed up, as you walked, although Auntie Aileen always said she couldn't see the tear. She loved the dress, kept asking me to parade up and down her room in it. She had no idea it was out of fashion.

Once she asked me if I was getting married.

Philip was there at the time, but he didn't say anything. Auntie Aileen liked it when he sat beside her, on a hard chair drawn up next to hers, with his neat pale hair and crisp collarless shirts and Canadian ease. He was her idea of a perfect gentleman, a sort of Transatlantic Richard Todd who could be trusted to drop bombs on the right targets and still write the letters to the grieving relatives; cool, capable, courteous. Two vertebrae in Auntie Aileen's neck had locked, and her head was permanently on one side, tipped toward her shoulder like a puppet with the strings gone slack. When Philip came into the room she'd twist the whole top half of her body and point at his chest and shake her head, as best she could.

It was a joke between them. Philip didn't wear a tie, because as an artist you don't need to wear one. Only he understood what she was getting at the first time she pointed at him, in a way I never could.

He made her feel safe. I could see it, the way when she laughed her eyes came back to the colour they used to be, like the eyes of the slaves in that Muppet movie The Dark Crystal. They weren't fish-eyes any more but they darkened, had pupils again. Only mine didn't. Then it was time to put the dress away.

The only other person who ever saw the dress was Alex.

Alex said he was lured to Sapphire by the hats. In those days he was quite a local celebrity. He was an entertainer, not just in the pubs but occasional Sunday nights at the Pier Theatre. He sang a mixture of hit parade ballads and songs from the shows for the old folk, but he started all his spots with Misty, which fitted pretty neatly into both categories. His voice wasn't a crooner's voice, it was more a whispery version of Roy Orbison: tuneful, a bit wistful. The motorcycle crowd at the Pier Head Bar thought he was a waste of space, but the ladies loved his little-urchin-lost look, loved the way he wasn't quite big enough for his clothes. He was like a pixie with his pale pointed face like a wedge of Dairylea poking from beneath the brim of a Sapphire hat, and his long mousy hair nicely washed and blow-dried. I say mousy, but there was a reddish tinge to it which got him the nickname Sandy at school, so when he needed a stage name that was it. Sandy Laine, because, as he told his audiences, Sandie Shaw had already been taken. He liked the pun and he liked the laugh it got him when he got up on stage, the first blow it struck against the men who looked at him like he was a lost mongrel, ready to be taken to the shelter and put down.

But he loved the hats, and he didn't stop at grey felt fedoras and trilbys and velvet numbers with cartwheel brims but carried on into the ladies' styles. His favourites were a satin straw with white daisies all round the crown, and a pale cream frothy tulle-and-chiffon wedding hat with netting spun round it like a sugary spider's web. Betty said he had millinery blindness, but she couldn't prise the wedding hat from him. Alex said it was his Misty hat, and he was going to wear it on stage. And, to clinch the point, he pulled the veil down and broke into an up-tempo rendition of *Love Grows where my Rosemary Goes*.

Betty said the song was inappropriate, but mainly because the hat was Auntie Aileen's, one of a suitcase-full I'd brought in after she died.

Only somehow, I don't know why, I was glad that Alex had the hat. I'd often think of him wearing it, blurred and soft under the spotlights, while Philip was telling me about his latest audition. But I'd never let on.

14

She's standing at the reception desk. Behind her, across the hall, the door is open into the bar lounge; in front of her, across the desk with its photo-cornered blotter, its piles of tariff and Special Offer leaflets, is a varnished wooden board fixed to the wall with rows of hooks screwed to it for room keys. Most of the hooks have keys on them, silver keys with jagged edges on silver key-rings, a white slab of plastic with an etched number hanging down from every ring.

Three of the hooks have no keys.

Lynn glances at the receptionist, who is on the phone, and back to the wooden board, squinting at the numbers. This is a game she recognizes, one she hasn't played for years but whose rules are chalked indelibly on a blackboard wedged somewhere at the back of her brain, rules as useless and permanent as her nine times table. She puts her luggage down, throws her satchel on the floor, scrambles the crepe soles of her Start-Rite sandals up the side of the desk, stretches out her arm for the key to her room; and the old porter who wears a ginger wig laughs at her, clutches his epaulettes with his white fingers and then opens his hands like a Black and White Minstrel, tells her that they've let her room out to a paying guest. He says this at least once a week, and she's never sure if he's really done it. She has to go to the top of the hotel to find out, her satchel bumping behind her up all those stairs, looking for the zigzag of light stretching down the final flight, the silver pin of light shining downwards from the empty keyhole of her door. That will catch her like a searchlight, expose her like a spotlight turned on her white face at one of her mother's card parties.

It doesn't happen. When she gets to the top of the stairs the key is snug in the lock, the way it always is. And Lynn is outside, gasping with the fright of it, afraid to let herself in, listening at the door. The more she learns the rules of the porter's game, the less she's able to work out how to win; just as she never wins the kind of guessing-game her mother likes to play over cut-glasses of sherry after dinner in the residents' lounge, for the entertainment of the guests. Pontoon, you know, like the bridge, her mother says, laughing; and invariably what Lynn sees is the image of a raft, drifting across the rapids in a fast-flowing river, both riverbanks well out of reach. Her mother's bracelets jangle as she shuffles the pack, as she flicks two shiny cards towards each sherry-glass on the felt table top. Twist, if you don't have twenty-one. She offers the extra card to each guest in turn, holding it up between finger and thumb, the chequerboard back of the card toward the player. She has the tight smile of a party magician who knows the trick, knows all the numbers.

Bust. Her daughter hates surprises.

The receptionist puts the phone down. She is a disinterested girl in an anonymous uniform of white blouse, black waistcoat and black skirt, asking if the woman at the desk wants a room. Lynn has shut her eyes, not sure if she's about to pitch backward in a faint, but she's nodding, so the receptionist reaches to the board at her back, finds a key, hands it to her.

Lynn opens her eyes. The receptionist notes that they are dark brown eyes, surprising with such light blonde hair.

'I want the turret room,' she says. 'The round room on the corner, right at the top of the hotel.'

She pushes the white slab back over the pink blotter towards the receptionist. The girl takes it, looks at the number, pushes it back again.

'That's what you've got,' she says. 'Twenty-one.'

This receptionist has no white gloves, no porter's livery, but she has a poker face. All front-of-house staff should have a poker face, her mother said. Good for dealing with complaints, with undesirable guests. Although things must have changed since her mother's time, with the tramp having snuck into the bar behind the two old ladies and helped himself to The Financial Times and a green leatherette sofa. His sunhat is just visible in front of the window at the far end of the room, peeping over the pink blanket of his open newspaper. At the near end there's a fire blazing - not a real one, the hiss of gas gives it away, but respectable enough flames below a white marble mantelpiece and a large pub mirror with a painting of a toucan in profile. The toucan is nearly falling off his branch under the weight of his smiling orange bill; beneath the branch is the slogan *Guinness is Good For You.*

She gets her breath back. Her father says the porter is a bit of a comedian, doesn't mean any harm, everything's got a joke in it except the tribble on his head, take no notice. He doesn't come upstairs with her, though. He goes back into his office behind the sugar-glass door and after a moment she can hear the crunch of the adding machine consuming the day's bills. No twist, she says, turning back to the desk. She won't take the extra card, she won't use the hotel's lift, which in any case only goes as far as the second landing. She starts slowly up the stairs.

Other things have changed since she last counted her way up these flights and landings - four flights, two landings, one of them at the top of the first flight, the other between flights three and four. Carpets, for instance. The

97

first flight is carpeted wall to banister in a vaguely Pugin-esque pattern on a red ground, reasonable quality, not too old, spreading into the wide landing furnished with a dark oak chest flanked by a pair of old mahogany chairs. A basket of chlorine-bleached dried flowers sits on an antimacassar in the centre of the chest. At the bottom of the second flight the red carpet gives out and a green hardwearing corduroy takes over, flattened in the centres of the treads, folds of loose carpet overhanging the sides. There's no light in the stairwell, just a blurry impression of stippled, anaglypted walls painted magnolia, walls that are rough to the fingers, as sharp as mussel-mortared shingle to the soles of bare feet. The banister too has been wallpapered, boxed in with hardboard that knocks hollow as her suitcase hits against it.

Up you go, her father says in the moment before he shuts the office door; and up she goes, up the dark narrowing spine of the building, away from the ground and the view from the single half-moon window that lights the second landing with its view of half a world, casting its panorama onto the wall opposite her like a camera obscura, with its curved orange-slice of sky, its flat bay, the headland, the arc of hotels. And then she's past the view and at the top of the last flight of old brown stair-carpet with a darker stripe at its edges, the carpet that leaves a strip of painted wooden tread on either side, the way all carpets used to do. The banister comes out of its hardboard casing like a dried walnut from its shell, a thin dark rail and plain pine spindles varnished with wood-grain paint. There are three doors at the top arranged like three sides of a hexagon. The centre door is painted white, and has the brass numbers 2 and 1 screwed into its timber. On the cross-timber are two old screw holes, about six inches apart, and an unpainted oblong where a sign (*Private, Staff Only, No Exit*) has been removed.

Her hands have started to sweat. She turns from the door and looks down the stairwell, her head to one side as if she's listening. Maybe for Phil's phantom voice, maybe for something else. Far below there's the sound of a door shutting, and a muffled conversation, like someone speaking under water.

Lynn puts her key into the lock. It sticks, so she tries again. Tries it half a dozen times, until she's hot and tearful, thinking of the stairs, of the porter, of her mother. In the end, gasping, she thinks of something else: the aborted lecture, the slit envelope, and the smell of old newsprint in her hands; and she stands back, slowly moving her hand down to her handbag, feeling the cool metal of the key inside.

Turn the cards over, her mother says; and very slowly she starts to lift the first one from the felt with a fingernail, her head bent almost down to the table top as she tries to see what's underneath.

15

Auntie Aileen died quietly. Not peacefully, as it said in the paper; I never could work out how they knew whether somebody was peaceful or not. But quietly, sitting up in bed wearing her blue angora bed jacket, staring not at me or Uncle Simon but at her toes with their uncut toenails, peeping out from under the blankets at the foot of the bed. There was a blind look about her, a blindness that didn't come from her eyes but from her mind. I think she was in pain, but I can't be sure, and if someone doesn't cry or yell how can you know? We talked to her but she never answered, she'd already gone somewhere else, letting whatever had been in her mind drain down into her body and following it, running down like rain, like a watercolour wash across the page. When the Co-op man asked us all to go up and pay our last respects with her she was still sitting up in bed with her hands outside the sheet and her eyes closed but softly now, limp, as if the Co-op man had taken all her bones away and without them she could rest. I stayed for a few minutes but I couldn't wake her, I hadn't been able to wake her for months, not really. But I stayed because what I wanted was some words, even a whisper, her last words I suppose, even if I couldn't tell what they were, I'd have plenty of time now to work them out and I could listen to them, the way I listened to my tunes on the jukebox, while the men were talking, telling me what to do, or whistling.

Uncle Simon did the whistling. He'd always been proud of his whistling, which he did properly, not hissing through his teeth but making an O of his mouth, shaking the notes through his tonsils like an opera singer. When I was small he used to whistle Colonel Bogey while we were walking down to the beach together, and I'd keep time by clattering my spade on the pavement. But that was years ago, and I hadn't heard him for a long time, not since Nicola, maybe even before that. Then, while the doctor was sitting on our sofa filling in all the forms he suddenly started up again, not whistling a tune exactly but more whistling in snatches, four or five notes at a time, like a bird moving from one tree to another, telling us he was here and then going silent. And then when the doctor had gone he went off to the pub, the very same day Auntie Aileen died, before they'd even zipped her up in her black nylon clothes bag and taken her away. After that it was every night, right up to the time when he said he wanted to sell the house and get a little flat. He whistled when he came in and when he went out, whenever he thought Philip was bearing down on him to lock eyes and insist on talking to him.

Philip was the one who knew what to do. He never exactly said, Leave everything to me, but he knew all about the practical things, who to phone, which certificates you had to have, he understood probate and chattels and dying intestate. Nobody expected Auntie Aileen to have made a will, and the house was Uncle Simon's anyway, but at the bottom of her glove drawer (Philip was amazed anyone still had a glove drawer), underneath the lavender sachets and the key to her jewellery box, there was a list of her dresses and hats and all her rings and necklaces, and at the bottom of the list it just said 'Megan'. For a while I was happy with the list and the things in Auntie Aileen's chest of drawers, unfolding brown folded receipts from department stores, trying a marcasite brooch and a green satin cummerbund and the turban hat with the little bow at the neck that she wore for church. I shut the bedroom door and sat cross-legged on the floor ticking things off the list while Philip made phone calls for Uncle Simon. I'd hear his voice come through the floor the way I used to when Uncle Simon and Auntie Aileen argued, but Philip's was a cool voice, not a hot one, cool with keeping his head when all about him and so on, cool with somebody else's business. He seemed to say *can't* a lot, or maybe it was the word I noticed most because of his accent. But at the time it never occurred to me that he was sorting my future out as well as Uncle Simon's. I made myself a little den, surrounding myself with Auntie Aileen's things, getting them out one by one, looking at them, touching them, making what I thought was peace. And Auntie Aileen had felt safe with Philip.

But as the days passed after the funeral I got less and less comfortable. I began to feel safer putting things away than I did getting them out, I'd have a heavy lapful of brooches and then suddenly I'd rush to get them back into the jewellery box, I'd unfold a scarf only once before refolding it. Finally I got to the stage of not even taking things out of the dressing-table, but just looking at them in their neat quiet layers, then pushing back the drawer. Slowly, so as not to hear the squeak.

And the dreams of falling started up again. The floor of the bedroom seemed to creak when I sat down on it more than it used to, it sagged under me as if the wood was thinning, as if it was weakening under all the vibrations that passed through it. Philip's voice got into everything, it was in my head like tinnitus, there was a scent to it that I could smell in Auntie Aileen's silky scarves and the sateen insides of her handbags. Not the kind of scent you'd expect from a lady's clothes, 4711 or lavender or even musty; but a man's scent, the scent of aftershave, blue aftershave in a clear glass bottle. It caught the back of my throat, made the egg inside it swell. As long as I could cry, the egg had shrunk and shrivelled up inside me like an old stewed prune out of its juice; but now I was quiet, quiet for hours and days at a time and the egg filled up again till it was hard black, an Adam's apple in my neck saying its man's name in my ear, over and over again. Somewhere, deep down in my stomach underneath the egg, I knew there was a pool of liquid, pink liquid and black liquid, trying to mix themselves together into another colour. This colour would be female, it would come out of me in a woman's voice, round and full of petals, with my name on it. Often, I thought of painting it, I thought of Nigel and his blues, but my paints were packed away in one of Philip's boxes, the cardboard boxes he'd started bringing in and leaving round the house. And even Nigel was just another male, getting his voice in the way of mine, he'd only tell me that pink and black mixed together make nothing. No colour, no name for the colour.

So I tried something else. I made myself go out of the house, away from Philip's voice, away from Uncle Simon and his daily games of Patience that were now spread all over the dining table, getting in the way of Philip's papers. I tried to retrace Auntie Aileen's steps, I went to the shops and the library and the park and wherever I went it was quiet, restful, not full of men. Auntie Aileen's church was a small one, old-fashioned C of E with dark mostly empty pews and blue and yellow embroidered kneelers propped on the rails between them where you could rest your feet. I sat in a pew at the back and hung my head like you're supposed to do inside a church and waited for Auntie Aileen's God to come and speak to me. I knew he was a comfort, because she'd always told me so. I saw her God as a scarf, a dark woollen being who would wrap himself softly around my neck as I sat there and ask me to talk; but he never came. The only person who came was an organist

103

dressed in choirmaster's robes with a pile of sheet music under his arm, who tapped his way down the aisle and slipped through the little gate at the end before getting up on his stool and practising *Here Comes the Bride* for somebody's wedding. I don't think he realized I was there. I'd never heard so much noise in a small church, the chords crashed through the organ-pipes like cannonballs, they rattled the water-pipes beside the pews like a bevy of plumbers.

I couldn't hear myself think. And then all of a sudden he stopped playing, he leaned back and put his hands on top of his head like he was resting them, cooling them against the white dome of his skull. The sound of the organ ran down, it slid away from the last note in the tune like a clockwork toy dropped on the ground. Once the pipes had stopped juddering I realized I could hear singing, quite loud singing, but not *Here Comes the Bride*, a different tune, different words. It was my voice, singing *Misty*, the way I'd learned it from Alex, the way I wanted to sing along and never could because the audience would hear me. By now the organist was looking at me, I suppose wondering whether to laugh, but I was listening to my singing, amazed I was in tune, but even more amazed at how loud I was, how my voice echoed through the church, hit the roof and came back down to earth steady, took me by surprise like a mirror in the floor. There wasn't a mirror really, of course, but when I looked into the aisle there were little chunks of stone scattered all over the paving slabs; black stone, like pieces of coal dropped from a scuttle. They were the broken pieces of my egg, smooth and curved on their outsides but jagged where they'd smashed apart.

Out of the corner of my eye I saw the organist sliding down off his stool and I stopped singing. The silence dropped like a cloth over a birdcage. I didn't wait for him to come and throw me out, I just bolted, with my hands up to my head and my fingers in my ears.

Philip said I dreamt the whole thing. He said it because it wasn't the kind of story he would believe. The part he didn't believe was the part about my voice. If it was true, he said, why didn't I sing something for him and prove it?

When Philip said this I looked closely at his eyes to see whether he really wanted me to sing. It was easy enough to find out whether Philip meant something or not, if you knew how to look at him; sometimes the blue of his eyes was a see-through, watercolour blue, sometimes it was opaque and acrylic, and this blue was flat and hard and definitely acrylic. I shook my head. The next thing I knew he was talking about hotels and flats and house sales and notice. We were sitting in the dining room, while Uncle Simon was out at the pub, and Philip had taken the opportunity to fan his papers out across the whole of the tablecloth, the tapestry one that Auntie Aileen only kept on when guests were coming. Some of the papers weren't legal at all. Papers to do with somebody's death are black and white and set out with figures and numbered paragraphs, and a lot of Philip's papers were glossy and coloured. There was a hotel brochure with a seaside photograph on its cover, another brochure printed on cheaper paper headed *Flats for Winter Letting*, and finally a leaflet from an estate agent with a colour photograph of a house paper-clipped to the edge.

Our house.

Philip's drawl had become very broad, the way it always did when he was acting. Pleasing the British, he used to say when anyone commented on it, they loved all those long vowels and post-vocalic *rs*, but the effect of the drawl was that you stopped listening to what Philip was saying, his voice became like an instrumental version of *Misty*, a time-filler, a tune with no words to it.

It was only because I had the pictures to look at that I realized that I had to start listening for the words again, that if I didn't prick up my ears I'd miss my name, the way I used to when they called the register in infant school. My name was there all right, but floating around in a kind of dismembered state, its five letters scattered like cards from a pack of Lexicon, lost in the mass of Philip's plans and arrangements. The house was being sold. In fact it had been sold, and the new people were keen to get in by the end of the month, so that they could start upgrading the plumbing and knocking walls down. Uncle Simon would split the proceeds, he would go and live in a flat in town, and I would go and live in another one. But because Philip couldn't get me anywhere suitable straight away, he'd fixed it for me to stay in a local hotel until he found the right place. He opened the hotel brochure and showed me a picture of one of the bedrooms. The bed occupied most of the picture. It was a double one with a canopy of red curtains over it and Philip said he hoped I'd like what he'd chosen, it was the best room in the place.

I asked if the best room had a name.

Philip didn't know what I meant at all. I said, like the Rose Room, or the Imperial Suite. A proper address, like 12 Primrose Avenue, so people would know where to find me. He said he couldn't see the point, the arrangement was only temporary, and the brochure didn't say, but he'd ask if I wanted him to. He made a note in his Filofax, but from where I was sitting the writing just looked like a scribble with no words inside it.

And eventually it dawned on me that my chance to sing had been my last chance with Philip, my last chance to be somebody he didn't think I was; that when I shook my head it was a promise of the way it was going to be. *Keep thee only unto him*, as if we'd really been married. Except I was the only one who'd turned up at the church.

Uncle Simon didn't want to say goodbye. After all, he was only going a couple of streets away, we'd be visiting each other all the time. But he didn't take any furniture with him from the old house, he said he wouldn't know where to put it, and I (temporarily, of course) didn't have the space, I didn't know where to put Auntie Aileen's things either.

The one person who did know, though he'd never even met her, was Alex. He'd be her caretaker, he said, making off with the suitcase of hats under his arm. And the word stuck in my mind, *caretaker*, more than Auntie Aileen's God, more comfort when you said it last thing at night. So in a way that was where Auntie Aileen ended up, not underneath a slab of stone with the dead people but shining under a spotlight in the Pier Head Bar, with the punters' smoke drifting towards her in the beam and catching in the cream netting of her wedding hat, the chiffon crown nodding up and down while Alex worked the hecklers and went through his routines. She never missed a show, he said, and though I couldn't sing any more I was grateful to him for that.

And in the end, of course, it was Alex who couldn't sing any more. For a while after his operation I didn't know what had happened to him, - I was here, of course, by then, still temporary as Philip never stopped saying, and then one night Alex turned up in my child's chair, knees tucked up under his chin just the way he always did, still remembering things, until I felt he was my caretaker now.

And it was together we remembered her, never thought of her as dead. Usually she was wearing her yellow cotton dress with the little bow at the waist, plodding down the beach in her flip-flops where the sand was softest, chasing the windmill from my sandcastle because the wind had caught it; and the windmill was bowling along in a brisk westerly, turning over and over, its points trying to stick in the sand, trying to stop it, every time it fell.

PART III

16.

Room 21 comes and goes. Sometimes there are twin beds with duvets and French scrollwork headboards, sometimes a double bed with a brass headboard and a Sanderson flowered bedspread. The dressing table fills the window curve. It is mahogany, with a pink satin skirt tied around its kidney-shaped body with elastic, a long skirt draped around its invisible legs and feet. First the heavy triptych of mirrors blocks the window; then it's light again. The alternative interiors flash on and off, depending which light switch you use: the white square one to the right of the door, or the brown circular one on the other side, with the bakelite mahlstick switch that has to be forced into submission. People too materialize and dematerialize. At one moment it's her mother standing at the foot of the bed, folding linen, or pushing square boxes wrapped in Christmas paper into a pillowslip, or pulling the mitred sheet from underneath her; the next it's a young woman in a dressing-gown with a glass in her hand and lines of charcoal mascara drawn on her cheeks. Finally there is Phil, sitting on the end of the bed, his hands clasped around one knee, explaining something to the person in the bed - the double or the single bed, its boundaries are unclear - behind him. As he speaks he looks forward, into space. His eyes are white, like the eyes of Michelangelo's David. The person he is addressing isn't Lynn. She only sees the front view of him, the view that faces her as she comes into the room.

She stretches her arms out, one either side of her, and presses both switches. The room is plunged into darkness, or maybe something has shorted out. This is all she can manage for now. The radiator is cold behind its pierced decorative cover, cold when she puts her hand on the glossy white bone of its shoulder. If she stays here she will freeze. She is glad there is a downstairs. She is glad there is someone downstairs.

She leaves her suitcase, still strapped and packed, standing upright on the floor of the room. She locks the door and descends back into the world, walking herself down the stairs carefully, like a convalescent, letting herself down into the warmth of the bar. The barman with his short-sleeved shirt and tartan bow tie comes to take her order. The bottles glisten in the fridge behind him, their corks pointing towards her, their labels out of sight. There are many more wines than there used to be. She orders the first on the barman's list, a Chardonnay, and makes for the vacant end of the tramp's sofa, which turns out to be not leatherette but a soft, suede fabric, stained here and there with the blots of various dark splashes of alcohol. In front of the sofa is a low glass-topped table with one of those old maps of the world illustrated in two hemispheres underneath the glass. Only the western hemisphere is visible at present, since the tramp is playing Patience, and his four columns of cards obscure the North Pole and most of Asia. With her left hand clasping the key in her pocket she holds out her right hand. She learns the tramp's name. She learns that he smells, unexpectedly, not of whisky or urine or even (not excessively, at any rate), cigarette smoke, but predominantly of Brut aftershave, which she recognizes instantly, despite not having smelt it for the best part of three decades. She shakes his cool bony hand, and smiles, and asks in her best deadpan lecturer's voice why on earth he's been following her around.

'And I think I remember you,' she says. 'You're Sandy Laine.'

Alex has an alarming smile. It is not so much that he has teeth missing, but part of his lower jaw as well, a dark red scoop cut out of the lower centre of the smile, where his bottom teeth and gums should be, a kind of soft cavern opening up a view to the smaller twin caves of missing tonsils at the back of his mouth, letting out the powerless vibrato of his speech.

She wonders why she did not notice this when he ate the ice cream.

'Guinness,' he croaks, and points at the mirror.

It's hard to know if this is an answer to her question or not. Quite soon she will have worked out that it is pointless asking Alex to repeat things. Whether she can make out what he says or not, the only thing to do is make the best of it, and fill in the words that are completely unintelligible. Soon she will learn to ask again, when he has had time to forget the question, and see whether the answer makes any more sense.

The barman arrives with the drinks. Alex takes his pint, runs his tongue round the inside edge of the glass to make a groove in the froth, and continues with his game. He is not playing it correctly. He adds cards to his columns in descending order of value: jack, ten, nine and so on, but instead of separate columns for hearts and diamonds and clubs and spades there are two columns for red cards and two for black, the suits mixed up.

Lynn points this out. He shakes his head and carries on, turning up the queen of hearts and placing her carefully on top of the king of diamonds, adjusting the queen's position so that the king's head is still visible above her. The king's head is turned to the left, his face in profile; at the base of his crown, almost touching it, what looks like an axe-head.

113

The queen stares not to one side but out at nothing, her head framed by its nun's bonnet with stiff starched wings, a hat that looks like nothing so much as a paper aeroplane flipped upside down and dropped on her head. There is a pucker of anger in the white space of chin beneath her bottom lip, a black mark shaped like a comma lying on its side; the mouth is held tight closed. The queen is like Lewis Carroll's queen, like her mother, eternally angry with a flat, two-dimensional anger that has no source, that lies like a steel pool of mercury underneath the floorboards. Organization makes a wonderful container for anger, and a hotel requires a good deal of organization.

And now her father materializes, telling her she is too young to be allowed inside the bar, saying that her mother runs this hotel like a military operation, and yet there are no battles to justify the preparation; or if there are, none with a visible enemy. The running of this hotel is more akin to a religion, a religion where the ritual has replaced belief. And there are so many rituals. Half-bottles of sparkling wine in the guests' rooms (on the night of arrival only), to be replaced by jugs of iced water on the second day. Three white chrysanthemums in every vase on the restaurant tables. The front door is locked at ten to eleven precisely. The years pass, but not her mother's love of ritual. When the strange practice of leaving sweets on pillows at evening turn-down becomes fashionable, her mother embraces it with gusto. She sees the sweets in jars before they are distributed at night, while they are still wrapped in their twists of cellophane. Hard sweets, always either red or green, that must be sucked dangerously until they are small enough to be swallowed. Gobstoppers, the porter would have called them, but by then he is long since retired, and she is home from university for the holidays, and too old for sweets. Throughout her reign, her mother will greet every single guest personally at the reception desk. The smile she prepares for them has no gaps in it, no way through her whitened teeth to the mouth beyond. The dark pink lipstick that she favours stains her teeth, sticks the top lip to them like ice. Lynn can feel the stretch of this smile, almost certainly the guests can feel it too. But they are here for days only, hours maybe, soon on their way.

When she is younger she tries to understand. She thinks she will understand when she is sent away to school, then she thinks she will understand when she returns. Nowhere is far enough away, nowhere close enough to home, to let her in on her mother's secrets. And because she cannot understand, she copies. Wherever she finds herself - in her turret room at the top of the hotel, in the dormitory at her private boarding school - she carries out her own rituals, arranging her bottles of bath salts and perfume and shampoo on the bedside table in a strict hierarchy of size, lining up pens and pencils from left to right along her desk-top according to the permanence of the marks they make: pencil, crayon, fountain pen, dip pen for Indian ink. Her possessions learn their places and do not move from them. Her idea of peace is a bed made neatly with the pillows smoothed and stacked one above the other on the counterpane, a counterpane like glass. But at night she has to disturb this arrangement and climb inside.

Perhaps this is why she sleepwalks, like Ruthie with her pink spiky hair and her fresher's cough. She walks in circles. Around her room, down one flight of stairs and up another, around the frosty quad at school, around her room. At school other people bring her back to bed, and she always knows that they are doing it. She resists. The house mistress is called, and later on the doctor, who prescribes without diagnosis, as doctors do in those days. When she is finally persuaded to lie down again she knows that there is someone lying underneath her in the bed, she feels the mounds of their body beneath her sheet like a featherbed of flesh and bone, she cannot smooth herself a place.

The girls at school are ready enough to sympathize with the sleepwalking, but something in the rituals she must perform silences them. She becomes an alien to them, and they to her. By degrees of cruelty, she learns that women are the gender least tolerant of difference, the gender readiest to expel the strange; that the sharing of experience that binds women into friendships must be, by and large, experience shared by the majority. She watches these girls seek friends the way they seek a mirror, a glimpse of a configuration of features like their own. When she comes back from morning break to find her pens and pencils scattered and thrown at random on the floor, and Joy Richardson and her friends perched on the cupboards that line the classroom, swinging their legs and watching for her reaction, she does not challenge them. She has to walk the classroom until every pen and pencil is accounted for, each one replaced exactly where it was, until the disorder that terrifies her has receded. At night, a few of them try to retrieve their position, sitting on her bed, asking questions about the doctor's pills, telling tales on their little sisters who also sleepwalk and wet the bed, but she is outside them, she holds herself aloof.

This is the closest she ever comes to any understanding of her mother. She walks for a time in her footsteps, as it were, but she does not begin at her beginning. There is something earlier, some prior part of her journey Lynn cannot see, a surprise still waiting to be sprung on her. And it is while running full-tilt from this surprise, that she falls into the hands of men.

Alex has turned up the king of hearts. Because of the way he has amalgamated the suits, there is no place for it, so he flicks it away from him onto the table, onto the western hemisphere of the world, somewhere mid-Atlantic, just to the right of her glass. This king has a doleful face, with heavy-lidded pensive eyes and a small crimped mouth; his neat, petite right hand is held in front of his chest, protecting the guards of ermine that edge his robes. Over his left shoulder another hand, or rather fist, rises up out of a raised arm. The fist grips a sword; the hilts and part of the blade are visible, but the point is hidden behind the king's head. This hand is ostensibly the king's left hand, but it looks disconnected from him, on another plane from the broad shoulder-line that disappears off the edge of the card. It is more like a beheading hand, caught in the moment before the execution, flourishing the weapon before it strikes.

The king's eyes dream on. He does not know what is going to happen to him. How she sympathizes. After all these years, fatally, she sympathizes.

Her time in the ranks of girlhood is over long before she leaves school and moves on to university. Already, in the fourth form, she is siding with male teachers against the tricks of her female contemporaries: even elderly teachers like Mr Eagleton (O level English), who cannot keep order, who have long ago abandoned the struggle with impertinent youth. The favoured strategy against Mr Eagleton's weary appeals for silence is a synchronized dropping of rulers onto the floor of Room 12; a noise amplified by the glossed floorboards so that it sounds in the classroom above like the slamming of desk-lids, or the crash of piano-keys, or the collapse of store-cupboards.

The only ruler that remains on the desk is hers. This is obvious to Mr Eagleton not so much when the rulers are dropped, as when the girls bend, sniggering into their shiny purple skirts, to retrieve them. She faces front, arms folded, and does not move. Even at the time, she notices how it is her folded arms, the fingers of the right hand splayed and empty against the sleeve of her purple cardigan, that draw Mr Eagleton's gaze; that not once, at any time, do they lock eyes. But at the end of the school year, Mr Eagleton leaves a book in her desk, wrapped in brown paper. This book is *The Shape of Things to Come* by H.G. Wells; not, as she expects, a juvenile War-of-the-Worlds type adventure but a dry-as-dust discursion on the future of society; an abstract tome about an idealized and faceless state, filmed once in 1935 and long out of print. Her copy has hard blue covers and thick, damp, closely-written pages bound too tightly to a fragile spine, concealing some of the words; the sort of book that cannot be opened too far without causing irretrievable damage. She examines the flyleaf for a message, and there is nothing except the rubbed-out remnants of a pencilled price. No name, no dedication, no date. But she believes in this book, in its significance. It is the first sign she can remember that is clearly intended for her.

Afterwards the world is full of signs. Nothing is what it seems, least of all is anything simply what it says. Every object in the world becomes the visible half of itself, the part that means something else. Only the invisible half is not a mirror-image of the visible one, rather it is the half that completes it, the half that is different; the shoe in the stockroom that is more real than the one on display.

It seems to Lynn that she too acquires an invisible half. One that is hidden even from her.

She is on a bus, on one of her periodic journeys home from university, when she sees the poster. The bus has stopped at the lights, and the poster is one of many pasted to the boarded-up wall of a dilapidated Thirties pub. It is a close-up of a man's face, printed in two colours: shades of black and blue, with the title of the play picked out in white and scrawled across the centre of the face. The man's eyes are pale, with tiny black pupils; his mouth is slightly open, the teeth set and even. Something terrible is happening around this man, but his face is unmoving. Its stillness is inspiring, it draws the eye upward like a marble obelisk aimed at the sky. It shines.

The lights change before she has made a note of the dates. But she has memorized the name of the theatre, and the next day, after she has unpacked, she goes to the box-office and makes enquiries. She is tense with the significance of the moment, but good at disguising it. She explains her interest in study of the text, of the adaptation of the novel into drama, and the next thing she knows she has been invited in to watch rehearsals.

There is nothing particularly remarkable in this. The production is a local repertory one - repertory still exists in those days - and audiences out of the summer season are hard to come by. Publicity by word of mouth being demonstrably free, she is provided with a sheaf of flyers and steered towards the theatre's black-carpeted stairs. The door is open, and she is about to walk through it.

Years later she wonders if it would have been the same, if another actor had been cast as Essenden, if someone else's face had been on the poster. In other words, was Phil's image part of the sign, or incidental to it?

Alex has tired of his game and pushed all the cards together into one haphazard pile in the centre of the table top. He rolls the pile out like pastry, with the heel of his hand, until the cards cover most of the glass. Then he clears his throat and takes a clean, neatly ironed hanky in a plastic packet from his pocket, removes the hanky and spits on it. He examines the spittle intently. She's started to think he

119

does not like questions. But more probably he just wants another drink.

'Last orders,' he grates, pointing at the clock beneath the toucan.

She watches the performance from the back of the auditorium, from an old-fashioned velvet-upholstered seat for two, which makes her realize that this theatre is in fact an old cinema. There is a small square window in the wall behind her for projection, the glass of the window now opaque and thick, like an eye dulled by a cataract. The stage in front of her is framed by red satin curtains, and by some appropriately austere scenery. A set of black flats protrudes from the wings, their line receding inward towards the rear of the stage.

The scene being rehearsed is from Wells' 'Melodramatic Interlude:' the deposition of the charismatic leader of the World State, Arden Essenden. It features Arden and Jean Essenden and the airgirl, Elizabeth Horthy, who stands with arms folded, in her grey flying suit at the front of the stage; she is looking out towards the audience, having just confessed her affair with Arden. Jean Essenden has collapsed onto the end of a bed covered by a black satin bedspread. She has her head in her hands, and wails, musically, rocking her head so that the spotlight catches the pale strawy sheen of her platinum wig. Arden stands at the back of the stage, in front of the projected image of his face, the same image as the poster, but magnified several times. The blue curves of the projection flicker across his face like expressions of anger or the marks of frostbite; when he moves forward the curves pass over him like waves.

Arden walks very slowly, but with purpose, towards the airgirl.

'Elizabeth,' he says, holding out his hand. 'Elizabeth.'

Elizabeth Horthy turns as he approaches her, and looks at him. She moves her head slowly from side to side, like a swimmer breathing left and right, the spotlight gleaming on her black glossy flying helmet. Arden steps right up to her and she backs off, dropping her thick black goggles across her eyes.

'No, Arden,' she says. 'I would do nothing that would harm the State. You, of all people, should know that. I will disappear, and no one will know where I have gone. Then it will be just you and Jean again. Everything as it was, before I came.'

Essenden withdraws his hand, carries it to his chest. From his breast pocket he brings out a small dark capsule, holds it up between thumb and finger for the airgirl to see.

'No,' he says. 'The Council have made it easy for me. I am instructed to go, alone, to a place I have loved in life and to take this tablet quietly, in my own time. All reproductions of my portrait will be destroyed. It will be as though I had never been.'

Elizabeth lowers her head.

'Not as though you had never been, Arden. The very air shudders with your presence. The closer I fly into the darkness of space, the more I feel it.'

Arden grips her arm, but she shakes him off and starts to walk slowly to the rear of the stage.

'What will you do?' he says.

Without turning, she raises an arm and points upward. As the lights dim, Jean Essenden's crying is the only sound.

Blackout.

As the lights go up, Lynn becomes aware of a woman sitting several rows in front of her in the stalls. While the rehearsal lasts, she is just a head and shoulders: a head with a froth of hair around it, catching the reflected footlights; candyfloss hair, fairground hair, nothing to be taken too seriously. When the curtains close she gets to her feet, shuffles to the end of her row and comes up the aisle. As she walks her hair swishes from side to side and a scent wafts from it, a low-tide, beach scent. Lynn watches her to the door at the back of the theatre, the double door that bangs after her. Only then does she turn, and see Arden Essenden still standing on the stage, a hand shading his eyes, looking down into the stalls.

Later she realizes that he sees her because of her hair. He calls down to her.

'Hi there. Do you have a minute?'

She nods. She has as many minutes as he likes. He joins her still in makeup, still in costume, which resembles Communist party dress of a decade earlier. It is severe, the cloth cool to the touch, as she imagines his skin to be.

He holds out his hand.

'Philip Arden. Good to meet you. Thanks for coming along.'

She looks at him.

'Really?'

'Really. It's a long story. How well did we do?'

For a moment she does not know what he means. He is looking straight at her, the pupils of his eyes expanding and then contracting, like a camera lens trying to focus.

'Oh, I see. No, I'm not a critic. I have a particular interest in the novel. It's an interesting adaptation, one that catches the period well.'

He takes a packet of Consulate from his breast pocket.

'I told them to stick with the future setting. 21st century. That's what the TV scouts will want. We could get a six-month series if the notices are right.'

She watches him light up. The scent of menthol drifts around her.

'The words, though,' she says. 'The words will be different in the future.'

He looks at her, not knowing what she means, enjoying it.

'I just learn the lines they give me. Haven't taken a prompt since college. Cigarette?'

He holds a single Consulate out to her between thumb and finger. The cigarette is white and slim and clean. His fingers too are pale, unstained, maybe bleached with the same liquid used to achieve the white sun-bleach of his hair. She hesitates. She does not smoke, has not smoked since school, since inhaling the fug of female secrets behind bolted doors in the toilets. But she takes the cigarette from Philip Arden's hand. She sees the steel flash of the lighter.

'Yes,' she says. 'Thanks.'

There is a flick of his thumb, a blue flame. A brief smell of burning.

Afterwards, she recognizes this as the moment when she falls in love, but at the time it is merely the moment when she forgets she's sitting in a cinema. While she listens to Phil's voice, while she draws in her slow smoky breath, remembering how to smoke, she watches him passing down a beam of light into solidity, she sees him becoming more than a sign. He is a symbol, beyond her powers of explanation, tough, residual, mysterious; a glimpse of the inexplicable world. Only much later does she relate the oscillation of his eyes to the flicker she begins to notice about him, the flicker that should warn her that he is not real, that there is no substance behind the projection. He is made up of still images, spun to give the impression of movement.

While she listens he does something he will do many times in the months and years ahead, he talks about the future, the roles he will have, the TV adaptation. There is a restfulness about his avoidance of the present. The chaos of the present is real, it is Here and Now. Phil tries to stay one step ahead of it by living in the future. At the time she thinks that this is reasonable, it is positive, above all it is wise; and, because wise, reassuring. Now she understands that the past and the future are the same thing, a way of being somewhere else, twin diversions around the chaos of the present.

The past and the future are projections.

Alex grunts. He has little patience with this sort of thing. He drains his Guinness noisily, sucking on the side of his glass, hoovering up the bubbles with his long grey tongue. Then he looks at her and says, perfectly clearly,

'Bedtime.'

She looks at him. Yes, she is tired. But before she can sleep there is one more thing she must tell him. She must tell him about her name.

It never occurs to her that she and Phil will not become an item, that they will not marry, although she is careful not to tell him about the blue book, about Mr Eagleton and her secession from the world of women. Phil is attracted to her as some men are to those they consider their intellectual superiors, with a mixture of deference and relief. Even when she gets her first lecturing job, he has no real idea of what she does, and he does not want enlightening. He likes to see what she is writing, dissertations, notes on research, conference papers, and so on, not to read any of it, but to see her name on the title page. Names are important, he says, they're what people remember. Phil's friends, most of whom are also in acting, have names like Loki and Nikki and Ran. Ridiculous names, names which condemn their owners to perpetual walk-ons in science fiction, to a silver-suited future.

124

She is glad Phil is not like them. Doubly glad, because his name is going to be hers too.

This happens sooner than she expects. Six weeks after they have started seeing one another, Phil whiles away a whole afternoon waiting for her to return from a research seminar by inscribing her name in all her books, taking them one by one from the flimsy white melamine bookcase in her room and writing in wet black ink on every flyleaf, blotting his inscriptions carefully with the blotter provided by her mother for the use of guests. When she comes home, she sees that her key is missing from the board in Reception. This is no longer the sign of a cruel joke, but merely an indication that Phil has arrived while she was out, and let himself into her room. On these occasions she is always nervous, she runs up the stairs like the schoolgirl she never was. She is worried that he will find something incriminating, something revealing, even though there is nothing to find.

On this particular day, as on others, Phil is smoking. Smoking out of the window, with the sash raised to its fullest extent so that the smoke blows out to sea, his hands on the windowsill and his body braced, like a man who has just glimpsed the three floors below him. As she opens the door he turns, stubs out his Consulate in the ashtray on the dressing table and tells her what he has been doing. She looks at her bookcase, but the books are all back in their places, neatly shelved, their spines lined up precisely an inch from the white melamine edge. It occurs to her how pleasant it would be to leave them like this.

'Thank you,' she says, giving him a peck on the cheek. Phil's complexion is English-Rose pale, but as a boy he must have had bad skin, because up close it is pitted with the empty craters of tiny blackheads, giving it the texture of lemon peel. Few people notice the craters, being

125

preoccupied with the luminosity of the hair and eyes. As he lets her out to arm's length the hair gleams.

'So,' he says, 'Are you going to look inside?'

She opens one of the books and reads the inscription. Then she takes down another book, and another. They are all the same.

This book belongs to Lynn Arden.

'Well,' he says, 'We're going to be married, aren't we?'

She touches the glossy writing, but the ink has dried. Then she looks up at him. The pupils of his eyes are pinpoints, the blue of each iris outlined in black, a thin black line holding in the colour like a sea-wall.

'Aren't we?' he says again, lighting another Consulate.

She doesn't know what to say. She stares at the book until the words finally harden into meaning. The oddity of what Phil has been doing lodges in her head like a splinter. At last she realizes that this is a proposal, perhaps the only one she's going to get, and she makes haste to give the right answer.

Phil moves in to her room. This makes sense, because he is waiting for the green light on the TV adaptation of the Wells play. *Green light* is part of drama-speak: amber means the project is ready to go ahead, the actors hired, the scripts learned; green is the release of the money. Once this happens he will have a regular income, and apartment-hunting can begin in earnest. Until then, the logical course of action is to share. She agrees, and makes space in the wardrobe for Phil's crisp, well-tailored clothes, his collarless shirts, the black linen jacket whose sleeves roll back to reveal a white silk lining with a faint black stripe. Her clothes squeeze up on the rail without a murmur. She tells herself that the movement is good for her, it will shock her obsessive personality into change. There will be a real body in the bed, one she can see.

126

The green light is a long time coming, just the way it is at traffic lights. There is a moment when the drivers waiting for the green believe the lights are stuck on red, a moment when they rev their engines and think about making a dash for it. But the lights must change, it's a question of patience, which is itself an act of faith. The problem is she doesn't know how to recognize such an act, having no faith herself. She takes Phil's word for it, all his words. She accepts his writing inside her books, a man's writing, upright and punched into the page, the words pressed on so hard that on the backs of the flyleaves there is a kind of ghost writing, white letters let into the paper like a braille version of the play-text, like the inscriptions on gravestones.

And only the backs of the flyleaves feel as though they're hers. *Verso* not *Recto*, the distaff side, the left-hand side of the bed. The side she starts to sleep on, rolled as far as she can go onto the left, her left arm curled under her, her bare left hand laid across her midriff.

'No sparkle yet,' her mother says. 'When do we get to see the sparkle?'

She slides her hand backward, to the edge of the desk, as if still a child. Despite living in the same building, she and her mother only ever really see one another when she goes downstairs to pay the monthly rental for her room. She notices changes in her then, the way one does in a relative one sees infrequently. She has grown older, her body dumpy and more dense, its outline hardening and retreating inward like a berry drying on the branch. There is less of her, and she is less able to hide the shrinkage. This is the moment when, if Lynn had grown into womanhood instead of away from it, like a plant growing backwards from a window into the gloom of a room, they might have made sense of one another. As it is, they stay the way they have always been, front of house, on opposite sides of the reception desk.

'Oh, quite soon,' she says. 'Phil is sketching the design.' She describes the ring to her mother, a platinum band with three stones, a central diamond flanked by two sapphires. Square stones, in a modern setting. Her mother nods and looks at her hand, but neither of them is fooled. There is no ring there, not even an invisible one.

Lynn lets go of the notion that Phil is her invisible half about the time he lets go of the future, of the green light, about the time he gives up circulating his Essenden portrait around TV producers and hides his face in radio, letting the listening public have his Transatlantic drawl and impossible vowels that give the Afternoon plays such colour. Only the visible colours are gone, there's just his voice stretching out into the ether, fading and crackling on the airwaves the further you drive away from the transmitter. He learns his lines in bed, on the right-hand side, propped on his right elbow and turned away from her, he learns them silently. And she sits up pretending to read and stares right through the door to where it says *The Round House* on the other side. There isn't any sign, of course, if there's any lesson she's well and truly learned it's that. And she doesn't sleepwalk any more, because Phil has taken the key into his safe-keeping. She must not leave the room, in case she can't get back.

She takes a breath and looks sideways at Alex. He doesn't look to her like a great reader, and he probably wouldn't have read much H G Wells if he was. He's been out of fashion for years, old hat, laughable and as faintly embarrassing as 1970s sci-fi; but in the novel Arden Essenden was the last personality, and when he was gone the government of the day became faceless, wars ceased, technology took off and took people into the air. Instead of faces they had aeroplanes, cold shining flashes of light in a pale blue sky, droning over them, dropping canisters of gas on their doubts and conflicts and intrigues, leaving them on the ground.

Of course, as they know none of this actually happened. Wars kept on breaking out, governments dispensed with ideology and went back to faces, aeroplanes either queued endlessly in the sky or fell out of it or were decommissioned on the grounds of cost. Only that, as Mr Eagleton knew, there's a sense in which the book is true. The future happened somewhere else, it went away and left them baffled, like a kite snatched from them by the wind. And it was up there somewhere, dangling its string, going on without them.

After the melodramatic interlude was played out and Phil was gone as well, for years she didn't think about it at all. She carried her sham name from the future around with her, she shut her briefcase on it like a silver ray-gun from her childhood. Phil was right about that, names are what people remember. And then one day she found herself with a key from a life that happened long ago, with ten minutes she couldn't account for. She supposes that's why she's here now, talking too much, trying to account for it.

So they had better leave it there and go to bed. As she recalls, there's a serviceable grey and white striped sofa on the landing outside her room, with a rather nice view of the bay. When Alex wakes up the sunrise will be hitting him full in the face, that and the seagulls screeching round the turret roof. And he can fill his pockets with anything he likes, except a pack of cards.

17.

The twin beds are both made up, when they get back to the room, but Alex doesn't ask for the spare one, he wants the striped sofa she's promised him, and she stands by the door in a white towelling bathrobe with *Esplanade* embroidered in red across the breast pocket and watches him getting ready for sleep. This involves him laying his moulting suede jacket and his white polo-neck carefully over the back of the sofa, then lifting up the seat cushions, taking off his golfing trousers and placing them underneath, neatly folded, before putting the cushions back. She closes the door on him and looks at the key in her hand, but she does not lock it. It is as if he's guarding her, and she puts her bag down on the bed and lies down. Drowsy, somehow for the first time in years.

She doesn't know the moment when she drops off to sleep, but at some point she dreams of Alex emerging from the bathroom, glistening with what she first takes to be water, but as he gets closer she realizes is oil, one of those freebie hotel bottles of scented oil he's smeared all over himself, Ocean Spray or something like it; a low-tide kind of smell, the smell of weary frothy waves lapping over the caddis worm casts, a mussel-encrusted, end-of-the-pier smell; and he gets into her bed without her ever feeling it, as if they were both underwater, and she turns her head, very slowly because of the weight of the sea on top of it, and looks at him; but now with the oil he looks as though he's been embalmed and she wants him out of the bed because already the sheets are dark with patches of it and falling into holes; so she nudges him and he rolls, surprisingly gracefully, onto the floor, taking one of the sheets with him.

Later in the night, when the world is turned down but not off, she wakes. She thinks about Alex sleeping out there on the landing, dreaming too of God knows what, and in the liminal state she's in she thinks he's knocking on the door and sits bolt upright, her breath coming loudly, listening. But it isn't him, it's a sound drifting up the stairwell from that other night years ago, a knocking that starts as a timid tap on the centre panel of the door, a little-bird-ish, long-fingernail kind of tap. Phil is well defended against the sound, lying on his good right ear, left shoulder blade punching the dark blue dawn; it's Lynn who hears the words, or rather word, *ill, ill, Phil, Phil*, letting itself through the keyhole in a voice that's like a shout, but an insect shout, the shrill pleading capacity of a tiny pair of lungs hopelessly out-voiced by a world of giants, like what's his name caught in the spider's web in *The Fly*.

She looks at Phil, but he doesn't move. Then she lies back and just listens. *Of course*, she thinks, of course, of course. The airgirl, the bathing cap, the girl with the sea-scented hair swishing past her in the stalls, Elizabeth Horthy's aeroplane plunging from the sky like a diver and just the sound of the wind passing through it before it hits the sea. *Philip*, it is, Philip, his whole name, she can hear it properly now. Over and over again, the same word, just the one word. This is the invisible half, his half, the other woman he's never let on about, voicing her claim at last. She could rattle the door handle, she could make a fuss, a scene, rouse the hotel, but she won't because she still loves him, and because a room is a fragile thing, easily taken away by someone else. The insect shout goes on and on but it's not loud enough. The only thing that will make him hear is if Lynn lets her in and they shout at him together.

131

And he's locked the door. Locked the door to stop her sleepwalking and falling down the stairs, although she's never sleepwalked, not since the day he moved in to her room.

She wants to shout, to explain that she can't open the door. Philip has the key, he confiscated it, like a prefect, like a teacher, he made out it was for her own good, he said he was concerned about her. If he told her where he'd hidden it who knows what might have happened? Her sleeping self would know the hiding place, she'd rise up like the walking dead and let herself out, fall through the void of the stairwell like an angel with frozen wings, like a pilot with no parachute. Now as she looks at Philip's back she sees the old porter with the wig, the man who's made himself the keeper of the keys but it's the joke he's really holding on to. Long, long ago she should have made her own copy of the key and put it somewhere safe, she's sure she has one somewhere but she doesn't know where it is.

She's getting out of bed to hunt for it. Her right leg goes over the side, and then her left. She's rolling out, away from him, she's going to let the insect woman in.

The key turns in the lock, she pulls the door open and stumbles through it. And then the floor comes up and hits her. She's fallen over Alex, wrapped in his sheet like a bony chrysalis, they're tangled up in the sheet together.

'Good morning,' he says, blinking with the heavy dose of sunshine in his face. For a moment she can't respond, she's winded with the impact of the floor, disoriented by the sound of screaming, which must be coming from her mouth, even though she can feel the pinned tightness of her lips, the wired hard set of her jaw.

'Seagulls,' says Alex, climbing out of the sheet and shaking himself free of it, going to the window to have a stretch and to take a look at the blue sky full of white wings, wings that don't flap but sail on the sky like gliders; not silent, because of the screaming. 'Just like you said.'

She starts to pick herself up and carefully, carefully, he peels away the sheet.

'Long day ahead,' he says, pushes past her and makes a rush for the bathroom.

She hears the sound of the water pouring in the shower and, after a minute, a faint, hoarse but pitch-perfect rendition of *Love Grows Where My Rosemary Goes*. The water's warm, she hears it in the song, she can see soapy rivers of it running down the bathroom walls, a sea-fog seeping out underneath the door, peeling the paint from the bedroom walls, dissolving them back into the unreal. The turret seems to sink under her feet, gently crumbling its way to sea-level like a slow-motion film of a collapsing chimney; and she goes down with it, also gently. Her suitcase tumbles with her, turning over and over and finally bursting open, spilling underwear and papers and, for some reason, a bucket and spade across the beach; but the case stays close to her as she falls, it's never out of reach because her whole life she's either packing or unpacking, her whole life she's lived in a hotel room perched on the edge of the bed like Jean Essenden, waiting for the sign to leave, for the next tenant to move in. Somewhere, on that other morning when she went off down the stairs leaving the door wide open, she knew that after the statutory gap of a few hours the cleaners would have swept the place clean of her, that the insect-woman would be sitting up in bed with mascara running down her face exactly where Lynn dreamed she'd be, with Phil's distant wordless voice uttering the explanation she was never going to ask for.

But this isn't that other morning. It's unmistakably a morning but a different one, an older one, infinitely longer ago. Sun and seagulls but other things as well, only half revealed, floating on the milky orange smudge of mist between land and sea. A time before the signs were painted on the doors, before the names were written in the books. Before Alex comes out of that bathroom, and it's time to leave.

18.

Alex seems to know where he's going. After breakfast, he pauses only long enough to fling leftover bits of toast out of the bar lounge window for the seagulls to catch as they drift by; then they're out onto the promenade and turning left against the wind, the headland looming up above them with pastel houses dotted around its slopes, white and pink and yellow houses with their own Victorian turrets, perched on the stepped limestone like hard-eyed nesting gulls. Alex drags her by the hand towards the Punch and Judy booth and the iron gates at the entrance to the pier, pointing with his free hand to the right, where the beach flows away from the concrete, where a huddle of donkeys waits at the slipway with their heads down.

'Bluebell,' he says, ratcheting his voice up a couple of decibels to be heard above the wind.

'That's right,' she says, staring at him.

He shakes his head and carries on dragging her.

'Dead now,' he says. 'Must be her daughter at least, or granddaughter. Everyone dies, or not quite everyone. You'll see.'

She digs her heels in and pulls back against him. He is surprisingly strong.

'Alex,' she says, 'Where are we going?'

He stops for a moment, pulls her backwards, and peers underneath the tent-flap of the Punch and Judy.

'Can't hear the children,' he says. 'No audience, no show. Same with the grown-ups. You'll see.'

Then they're off again, running for the little bus before it starts another trip around the headland. Lynn forbears to mention that she has made this journey already, and pays both fares without comment. As before, the bus pitches and tosses its way along the rough road until it nears the optional stop at the church. Just before the pull-in, Alex lunges forward and hits the red button within its chrome shell. The bus jerks to a stop.

They tumble down the steps onto the gravel path, up the grassy slope towards the iron gate that leads to the churchyard. There are actually two gates, set into an ornate iron arch with a small bell suspended from its apex. On summer Sundays the vicar rings this bell to call the congregation to worship, there being no bell tower on the church.

Or he used to. There is a wind blowing, but the bell appears fused to its housing, the clapper hangs motionless above her. She considers reaching up her hand, but decides against it.

Alex opens the half of the gate with the latch and pulls it back as far as it will go. Then he starts on the other half, the half that has grass growing round it, the half drilled firmly to the ground with a rusted iron bolt.

Lynn goes up to him and shakes his shoulder.

'Alex, what on earth are you doing?'

He shrugs her off and gets both hands to the bolt. It grinds in the socket, rasping against the iron barrel buried in the ground.

'Only half open,' he says, gasping and coughing. 'That's no good.'

She watches him for a moment and realizes he is not going to leave it.

'Oh, for Christ's sake,' she says.

She puts down her bag on the damp grass, bends and gets her hands under his bony fists; together they pull. All at once the bolt shoots out of its housing with a shower of red rust-sparks and they stumble backward. She attempts to keep her footing, fails, and falls on one buttock against a grassy bank.

Alex is inordinately delighted. He pushes up the brown sleeves of his jacket and hauls the reluctant half of the gate over the grass and nettles. The hinges scrape with the sound of an untuned violin and Alex sets up a wail in a reasonable approximation of the note. Then he takes off along the grass path that runs between the graves, turning left at the first branch. She follows him slowly, because now she can see which grave he is making for. As she walks, the dates carved on the stones roll forward from the distant to the recent past like the clock on a time machine. As with the dates, so the fashion of the gravestones: Victorian white angels and draped urns give way to mock walls of grey dressed granite four or five courses high, like abandoned buildings. The granite walls give way in their turn to the ghastly, gleaming rows of modern polished black stones. These slabs are atheist graves, and as both child and adult she loathes their emptiness. Curiously, or so she thinks at the time of her father's death, it is the Victorian style of monument that appeals to her. By the time her parents are both dead, statuary on gravestones has become almost a lost art, but statuary is what she is determined she will have. Her decision seems quixotic, but it is absolute. Something in the shape of human, something other than words, perhaps. Something other than a blank space, waiting for the words to fill it. Her angel is a guardian, a caretaker, standing where she cannot stand, where she cannot bring herself to stand. She chooses the design, pays the bill with money from her father's legacy, and leaves.

She sees the angel now, a white ghost standing knee-deep in black marble slabs, not fading like a ghost but resolving, like a mountain throwing off mist, as they get closer.

Alex waits for her, taking up a mourner's stance at the grave, his blue velvet hat in his hand. As she reaches him he turns and looks at her. The blue of his eyes is wet, concentrated, an undiluted pool of ultramarine.

He squats down to black marble level and points at the inscription.

'Lynn's mother,' he says, looking at her.

'Yes,' she says.

'And father.'

She nods. He reads the letters with his fingers, saying the feel of them.

'Of the Esplanade Hotel, North Parade. Ever in our thoughts.'

He gets up, knees creaking, moves close enough to whisper in her ear. He points again to the angel and then, oddly, at himself.

'No wings,' he says.

His breath has a cool touch, like menthol, slipping the words into her ear. They're strange words, somehow clean, somehow free of the act of reading. She feels as light as air. The angel looks through her veil into Lynn's eyes, her white eyes heavy with their thoughts, the thoughts she has been keeping for her. They are safe inside, they are intact. On the periphery of her vision Lynn sees the shadow of her invisible wings, dark as the wings of cormorants held up to dry on the rocks below the headland, dark around the limits of her sight like the queen of hearts' flying bonnet. She looks at the empty vase. The seasons run backward, scudding through her mind like clouds, one year ending, the next beginning, as she comes back to visit.

Once she is at university, she comes back with the seasons. She does not live there any more, she does not belong. For the first few years after her mother's death she brings flowers. She stakes her claim, for the length of time it takes the water to dry out, for the petals to wither and blow away. In the autumn, before term begins, she brings chrysanthemums. At Easter daffodils, in the summer vacation roses. And in winter, the dead red flowers meant for Christmas arrangements. Poinsettias, florid opium poppies with their black thready centres. By spring the silk petals are shredded, the colour bleached away by the salty gales. The thick green plastic stems, rammed too deep into the vase, have to be cut away.

Finally there are no flowers. They die, there is no point. The stone vase stays. She is afraid of the emptiness of it, and does not go back. Not for years, not until now.

But now has become now, and then, and - there is no one word for the future, no word that points at it in a single syllable.

The shape of things to come.

But there is no shape. Just the formlessness of a surprise, a secret, because they are one and the same thing. Springing out at her.

Under the base of the vase the white corner of a note pokes out.

'Someone comes here,' she says.

She bends down and picks up the vase. The stone is heavy, the metal insert full of water. From the damp shelter of the base armadillos scuttle away. Underneath is a square of white fabric, an embroidered handkerchief. Alex smiles, showing his disgraceful teeth, holds out the hanky to her.

'Megan comes,' he says.

She looks at the damp fabric, but does not touch it. It's still a white surface, white and blank to be filled with words. Not whole words here, but part of a word, the vital part, an initial. What is missing lies in the white space around the initial, the phantom words are the real message, the words rushing into the void her mother left her. There were always words between the lines, words hiding in the white space, invisible but she knew they were there. Meaning between the lines, it's called, a whole discipline of its own, and she knew how it was done before she ever started. Only there has to be something to work with, something more than nothing: a string of words, a single word, an initial. It means something else, always something else. Meaning is an escape from the silence of things, but its words are not the same as a voice. At home she left behind a blank, a nothing, a place where the words should have been but weren't, where the meaning doesn't even touch the word, white space where there's nothing left, an empty gravestone, a blank page.

Her mind flips her back to the lecture hall. Not weeks ago, but a handful of years. She feels the wave-sound of the air conditioning, the cold blast of the sea around her face. She's in a room with new windows, where the walls are brown varnished timber, where the seats rise in rows above her. She looks down, as always, and there it is, an envelope, a square of white paper in her hand. It's a letter, no, a telegram, with all the connotations of that word, connotations Ruthie and her friends have never known, just as they hardly know what a telegram was. She has a folder open on the lectern in front of her, she is about to speak. The lecture is a new one, so she has written all her notes out in longhand, notes she will not alter for twenty years. The telegram is short. Two words, four letters each.

Come home. Nothing else.

She returns home on the train. In those days there are still trains, good ones where you don't have to change, although the train is crammed with holidaymakers. She shares her table for four with a young couple bound for

Rhyl. The part of her she has left behind at university, the part Phil claimed in the flyleaves of her books, silently mocks the woman's cheap seashell necklace, the fluorescent pink of her nails, her golden clock-weight earrings, each the marking gift of a holiday. She smiles, admires the jewellery, does not quite lie. When they get off she is close to panic, spreading her belongings over the empty seats.

In the eighties the hotel has a wrought-iron front gate set into the wall, a little like this one, with a light at the top for guests returning late. When she reaches it, a little after eleven, the light is out, but the lighting from the hall shines through the panels of the front door. The door is shut, with a note pinned to its central panel.

Closed due to family bereavement.

The door is locked. She rings the bell and steps back, lets her case down in front of her. The words on the door are vague, blurred like objects out at sea but drifting closer. She can see down the length of the hall to the reception desk where her mother always would sit between the hours of two and five, just the top of her fashionable red wig showing like a sea anemone above the desk as she waited for the phone to ring, for her guests to arrive. Finally someone, a receptionist Lynn does not know, and who does not know her, answers the door, and she explains who she is. The girl stares at her and turns, calling her father's name.

She listens. There is a distinctive, familiar sound, reminiscent of the sound of someone peeling potatoes.

'It's all right,' she says. 'I know where he is.'

She goes up to the reception desk and looks through the open doorway to the office beyond. He's sitting with his back to her, his hair-oil gleaming as from a dip in the sea, his right hand working the adding machine, a roll of paper uncoiling around his knees and pooling on the floor.

After a minute she rings the bell on the desk. He hears it, but he does not turn.

The next day they will talk. Now, in the moment, in the present, neither of them can speak.

In the dining room the cloths have been swept away and the tables stand just as they are, pine legs topped with circles of chipboard, legs with knots of darker wood on them like birthmarks, like the marks of age.

In the coffee lounge the writing desk is open and her pen left with the top off. All the pigeonholes emptied. Just a block of writing paper with the hotel name at the top. Her mother's diaries, Lynn's last hope of understanding her, are gone.

All her words. Women's words.

She looks back at her angel. She's willing her to speak, but she won't. Her beauty is broken off below the mouth, just a sliver of it, a piece of her jaw gone missing, taking an edge of mouth with it.

As the images run through her head, one after another, she hears the click of the projector. She knows where she is now, back in the lecture hall, in the middle of her silence, a newspaper cutting and a key in her pocket. She knows what she is going to say.

The projector stops. There is a colour in her head.

'Megan brings poppies,' Alex says.

She looks at Alex. She holds her hand out to him.

'You brought us here.'

He sniffs and wipes his hand on a damp sleeve.

'Lynn had to come. You'll see why.'

She nods.

'Take me to see Megan,' she says.

19

They're back on the promenade, standing by the war memorial, facing inland. Behind the tall white obelisk the road cuts a straight line right through the centre of town to the bay on the other side of the peninsula, giving a clear view through to the west shore and, beyond the further bay, a grey hump of hills heaving out of the flat line of sea. It's the reverse of the view on Lynn's postcard, because now the Esplanade is on her left, the pub and older buildings on her right, but the real difference is the absence of sea, the real change is what seems to be a looking inward, not outward. On the steps of the obelisk are the usual collection of poppy-day wreaths, left there for God knows how many months because nobody will touch them, left there until the red silk whitens in the onshore breeze and one day, out of season, a council official comes and whips them quietly away. They're anonymous, part of a ritual, somehow comforting, everyone's and no-one's. She used to come here to cry, it was a place where you could cry and nobody would question you, a safe distance from the hotel, from her parents' grave, from her wingless angel.

For a while she could summon up a few tears for people she'd never met. Then not even that.

There's a tug from Alex.

'Come on, Lynnie,' he says. 'Enough dead people for one day.'

He's right, of course. She's beginning to realize that he's almost always right, that he's closed in on her without her even realizing it. So far, but maybe no further. Right now she's standing on the right-hand pavement and the pub sign is swinging over her head. For one disorienting moment she sees herself as from a window far above, her coat collar turned up, her bag clutched to her side as if she fears a mugger, her left hand out of sight behind Alex's back. She sees from the perspective of a part of her that does the seeing, a part down there that lives and breathes and moves through life. Then the seeing part is gone, and there's just the pub sign with its king's head, a king of diamonds like the one on the card, his profile looking out across the road with its red and yellow and black crown, his ermine collar warming his thick neck.

And no axe aimed at it, or not one she can see.

The pub door, like the graveyard gate, is half open. Inside she can't see very much, just the edge of the bar and the pumps with their names picked out in neon. *Courage, Strongbow,* and of course *Guinness.* She imagines a few all-day punters sitting back in the gloom, the sort of surrogate family Alex might have, sharing beer-money and greasy hats and the odd needle. If they're there, they're not talking. All she can hear is the thump of darts hitting a board.

Ralph Anthony Reid, says the sign over the door, a sign that has been painted over many times until the paint has acquired a softness, a viscosity of thickness, the deeper layers have never dried. The whitened-out ghosts of other letters, the moist forms of other names lurk beneath this name.

She stops in her tracks.

'No,' she says. 'No.'

Alex drops her hand. This time he doesn't say anything, he's taken a sudden, unexpected vow of silence. His mouth is closed, his arms folded across his chest. He's waiting. Something rises up in her throat, sour as vomit. She's angry with him, angry with him for being real, for resolving into a person before her eyes.

She hears her voice, croaking through the vomit or the tears or whatever it is that's down there, shaking. A mouse voice, like hers, like the Incredible Shrinking Man.

'I feel as if he's in there,' she says. 'Phil. In there, waiting for me.'

Alex knocks on the half of the door that's shut and then steps back, waiting for her to go in first. She moves in sideways, shuffling her feet across the threshold, letting the pub darkness swallow the blindness of the light outside.

Her eyes darken with the interior, until she can see. She's inside, and he isn't here. The adrenalin shot that's brought her this far runs down. The ground rushes up to meet her, as if she jumped from a plane without a parachute.

Inside the bar it's cool. A cool gloom, like the inside of a church, only spiced not with incense but with a beer-smell, a disinfectant smell and something else, like varnish, hairspray, a glue-sniffers' kind of smell. There appear to be no chairs, but a long padded seat runs around three sides of the room, upholstered in green plush fabric, rather the worse for wear. Two large dark wooden tables, their timber distressed into assumed age, block the few customers into their corner seats. One of the far corners is empty, the other occupied by a man and a woman in quiet conversation. The man mostly just drinks his beer, but the woman talks with her hands, her long pink fingernails glinting when she laughs.

She can't see the dartboard, but she can hear something. Piped music, turned down so it's hard to hear if you don't know the song, a woman's voice. Dusty Springfield, singing *Goin' Back.*

'You know the words, Lynnie,' says Alex's voice blowing on her cheek.

Her ear is becoming accustomed to him, so that although she jumps, it is not for that. For being seen, she supposes, for being heard.

He grins at her and lets out a howl. The woman with the fingernails looks up, tells him amiably to fuck off. He offers her the two fingers of peace and love, then grabs Lynn's hand and starts to shake it.

'Dusty, Dusty,' he says. 'I'm Sandy. Pleased to meet you.'

The barmaid laughs. She's leaning on the bar, arms folded, fleshy in a skimpy top. She's wearing large hoop earrings and a charm bracelet that jingles when she moves. Her hair is bottle-black, shoulder-length, crinkle-permed, but the face looking out of it is not the masculine, bruiser's face of so many women of her type. It is a woman's face, a woman of the old school, before school wiped such women out. A woman like a middle-aged version of the Shrimp, a Dusty, a dollybird. She is the kind of woman who belongs in one of the kiosks along the pier, her lacquered hair hot-tonged into waves, staring out at nothing under the black bar of her eyelashes, selling small feminine souvenirs: wind-chimes, embroidered handkerchiefs, boxes made of shells. Lynn feels a hot rush of envy of her life, an unspoken rage, as if she were a man who has gone out to work while his wife stayed at home, indoors, staying behind the curtains with a white face to match.

The barmaid begins to pull a pint of Guinness.

'Alex got himself a marriage made in Heaven at last,' she says, and the wind-chime is in her voice, lifting her final syllables. 'What's yours, dear?'

Alex leans on the bar.

146

'This is Pauline, Dusty. Dusty's come to see Megan, Pauline. Where's Megan?'

Pauline looks at her. The look has in it all the years of staying put, of stillness, an unawareness that there is anything outside.

I remember you, Lynn can hear her thinking. *The girl from the Esplanade.*

'I can't serve him. He's barred, but I can serve you,' she says. 'Chardonnay, is it?'

She doesn't answer straight away. She's scanning the walls of the room, looking for a door. It will be a door that opens towards her, stiff and swollen in its frame, a door that she must pull as far as it will open, one that she has to get around. She moves slowly away from the bar, into the chair-less room. For a moment she's adrift in the centre of it.

Alex slides down from the bar.

'Can't see the lord and master,' he says. 'Where's the lord and master, Pauline?'

The barmaid offers up a glass of white wine.

'God knows,' she says. 'That'll be seven-twenty, please.'

Lynn turns, goes back to pay her, takes her wine and goes back again to her place in the centre of the room. Her feet feel shoeless, twitchy, following something in her mind, her toes feel the groove between the floorboards, the tacky cling of beer-spills. The door is right in front of her, where the green plush ends in a scuffed armrest; a stripped-down door of pine with frosted glass in its upper panels. *Residents Only,* it should say, but there's nothing there, and the voided words give her courage. She feels as if she's sleepwalking, out in the dark room beyond her room, making her way back to bed. Through the frosted glass are the stairs with their dull orange fitted carpet, above them the skylight with its half-moon of light, and beyond them her room with its bed.

She gets hold of the brass doorknob and pulls hard. Nothing happens. She pulls again, harder, and it's just the same. She doesn't turn round, to see what Alex is doing, if she turns round now she will wake. She tries again, sweating hard. The door is becoming unreal, already fading. She has to get through before it disappears.

She looks down at her hand, red and angry around the doorknob. Beyond this doorknob, its image fed back to her in reverse though the milky glass, is another doorknob, and a sea-washed, blurred version of her twisting hand beyond it.

And then the penny drops. She's forgotten the mirror effect. The door opens the other way.

Her right hand turns to the left and the latch disengages. She pushes. The stairwell opens up in front of her, stairs scraped clean of carpet, streaks and threads of colour left on the treads. The route to the top is a tunnel through cascades of wallpaper, half-stripped and hanging in damp rags from the walls either side of the stairs, from the low stairwell above them.

Up you go, her father's voice says, and she does, her feet still taking her, still knowing where they're going. At the top it will be familiar, she will know where she is. And she does.

There's nothing much on the landing, just the phone and the message board where girls leave names and numbers and their boyfriends' names scribbled inside pierced hearts; the phone receiver hangs from its black curled cord, muttering static; she replaces it, out of habit, as she passes. Her mind is skipping through time, flashing between the pub landing and the dormitory corridor at school: she sees three bedroom doors on the right, all open, but nothing of particular interest inside: typical girls' rooms, one shared washbasin underneath the window hoisted up on a framework of chromed metal, two single beds pushed back against opposing walls, walls papered with the folk-heroes of the day: James Dean, Jim Morrison, Tim Buckley. In the third room there's a girl lying on the bed reading a comic, probably *Jackie*; her ankles are crossed and her feet in loose beige concertina socks wave gently in the air. Her transistor radio is on, a red stippled affair with a gold dial and a white plastic carrying handle, with *Pye* written on a small crest in the centre of the dial. She's listening to the great-208, and singing along to a popular number by Edison Lighthouse. Lynn passes without attracting her attention.

The further she goes, the stronger the smell gets. Less the thin smell of hairspray now, more varnish, more the heavy, heady smell of paint that seeps in through your pores and runs upward to the top of your head.

When she gets to the fourth door she finds the source of the smell. The door gleams softly with fresh pale blue eggshell paint, dry to the touch but pungent with the thickness of the coats beneath. She feels as if the surface would yield if she pressed it, leave a perfect mould of her handprint, a record of her attempt to enter. The paint has been carried over from door to doorframe as with a single stroke, the thick viscous brush full hardening across the gap.

She tries the door. It sticks, so she pushes harder. The resistance is both hard and soft, hard with the steel slab of the engaged lock, soft with something else, a dense plastic resistance like bubblegum, stretching and giving but clinging long after all its sweetness has been sucked away. The bubblegum she hated, sullen and solid in her mouth, never able to learn the trick of blowing the spheres of

149

transparent pinkness that burst and smacked back against her fellow pupils' lips.

She is accustomed to locks. She feels in the pocket of her coat for a key, and when she finds one it doesn't surprise her as much as it should. It turns in the escutcheon and the slab of metal shoots back, but the door doesn't open.

She's pushed again several times before she realizes what it is she has to do. She needs to get her shoulder to the door, thrust her whole weight against it, lean right in to the sticky blue surface, and she wonders if she's going to do it. Behind her when she looks the imaginary Luxembourg girl has come out of her room and is standing on the landing watching her. As Lynn turns she stretches out an arm, grabs the receiver off its rest and leaves it hanging, the way it was when she came up the stairs. Come and get it, her eyes say, come and get it and I'll do it again, as many times as you like. There's no way past her, no way through her. The torn wallpaper sways like seaweed, tangles the way downward, the way back down the stairs. Lynn shuts her eyes, forces herself back to the here and now. She has to reach Megan's room or she'll never really wake, this room she's come to because it's so much like her own, because they share not only the memory of a dead man but a grave that might have been his but isn't; and there's no way out for either of them any more but through each other, through this door that, in the nature of doors, must open somehow and so she turns her shoulder to the sticky surface and barges it. Not once, but several times, so the sound reverberates along the landing, so the other doors bang with the vibration, so the boards creak and snap. With every barge a tiny gap opens up between door and doorframe, a gap with thin dark splinters in it that she takes to be broken bits of timber before she realizes that they're paint, black paint applied not

150

from the outside but from the inside. The splinters don't stretch like bubble-gum but flake and shatter, as if they're older paint, the kind of paint you find on wood after you've stripped down all the layers of years past, the kind of paint that doesn't strip but melts into a glutinous liquid that never quite dissolves. As she pushes the splinters fall in showers round her feet till her toes are stinging with the sharpness of the floor, but finally she can see inside, or at least she sees something beyond the splinters, a greenish light, and she smells a waft of air brush-laden with paint but with the green smell of sea as well, a breeze blowing from an open window.

One final barge and she's in, the remaining paint pulling away with a sound like firecrackers, like a shower of bullets. She falls into the room, face-down on a rug, her skirt up round her ears. In front of her face is the trailing end of a lilac quilt. She reaches a hand out and beyond the quilt is a mattress, and the hard brass bedstead of a bed. Slowly she pulls herself up the bedstead, hand over hand. When she's almost upright she sways forward, steadying herself with her free hand on the bed, letting the billows of quilt take her weight.

Another smell slips through the paint. The sweet smell of rosemary.

She feels something, someone, through her tingling fingers. The hardness of bone, of a body underneath the quilt. She wails like a banshee, enough to wake the dead.

There's somebody in the room. I jolt awake and for a moment I think it's Philip coming back to bed, he's climbed in quietly so as to surprise me, but then I hear the breathing and I know that it's not him. Something's happened to the air, it's not the cool green smell of paint

151

any more, it's something broken through the door, something that shouldn't be here if it's just him and me. I need him but he's late, he should have been home by now but I feel the quilt getting cold and slippery as if I've been lying here too long.

And there's a hand on it, a woman's hand. I feel the nails through the softness, nails like Nicola's hand, like the convention women, nails that dig through my sleep. I keep my eyes shut but I see her just the same, I know who she is, the woman I saw at the window of the room that should have been mine, that day Philip brought me here, put Auntie Aileen's old cases down on the red bedcover. The day I stared out of the window at the Esplanade across the road with the turret room lit up like a castle and saw her, blonde hair in a ponytail, standing in the light with her back to me.

The day I said to Philip, I thought I was going to live over there.

It's just temporary, he said, and he was pulling out my things from the suitcase and spreading them across the child's chair and spraying the room with my yellow perfume until the walls ran dark, and when the smell had settled on the floor and I saw how the hard lines of the room were rubbed out by the softness of my Sapphire dresses it didn't seem so bad; and by the time I looked out of the window again she was gone.

Now I want to ask him why she's here, why she took my room, why he isn't here with me because I'm lying here all alone and listening to the words she's putting inside my head. Bits of sentences, words that don't make sense, words about doors and keys and death that I want to blur but they pour into my ears and run right down inside my body, to the place where I keep Quetzal curled up tight and safe; and I feel as if she's melting, softening in the rain like the angels in the graveyard on the headland, dripping and running out of me. The blonde woman's words go on and on as if she's afraid to stop, that if she does the death and leaving will get her too. But it's me they've got, and suddenly I know I'm losing Quetzal and I scream for Philip and he isn't here.

Not here, but I know where he is. And I drag myself up and the quilt falls away from me and the cold seeps into my stomach and there's no hot water bottle there. There's her, in my room and out of it, in the room I should have had, in my place with Philip.

And the door is open. I went over there, I called for him. I hear my voice, calling, echoing in the stairwell. But the sound feels far away, as if it was years ago.

I saw you once, Lynn thinks. *In a theatre, the day Phil and I first met.* She realizes that now, she thinks how their lives might have run straighter, happier, if they'd known one another. But they have to go to the end, if Alex has taught her anything it's that. They have to put their lives back together until they're whole, not two halves that don't recognize each other, can't tell the past from its projection into their present, what's years ago, what's now.

But right now it's years ago again, and she's back in the turret room with the insect-shout in her ears and she's shaking Phil's shoulder. She's done this before, sometimes when she can't sleep for his snoring, but more often when he's talking in his sleep. He takes the shaking as a prompt, the prompt he says he's never had. Sometimes he delivers only snatches of lines or the odd name but this time the shaking is hard enough to set an entire scene going, the one that fits, the one that's almost real except for being set in the future when it should be the past.

153

He's lying on his side. Right side, facing the window, right arm crooked and forearm held across his eyes against the light, his shoulders woman-white, smooth and hairless. His breathing is heavy with the vodka he drinks in the studio bar, the vodka he doesn't bring home, just the day's voice-work, the words in bundles, the radio that doesn't let his face be seen. His face has become unused, it's set into the poster portrait in black and blue, the place where she first saw him; set into the stare that's looking inwards. The colour from his eyes drained back almost into white, back almost into blindness. He'll stumble up the stairs, knock against the bed. The only way he still seems to see is when he's looking out the window smoking, looking not out to sea but back across the road, not dreaming of the future but talking his lines back to himself, listening for an echo.

Or not an echo. She hears it too. She shakes him hard enough to start the play-scene moving in his head, for him to see not her but Jean Essenden, sitting on the bed and crying, poised and beautiful with her gloss straw hair but both of them know she's never been enough for Arden. It's Elizabeth he's been seeing all these years, Elizabeth he's been keeping from his wife, behind his eyes, behind a locked door like the first Mrs Rochester. His head twists so he's looking down the bed at Jean, he's shaken hard enough to talk to her. She knows the words by heart, she's heard them all before.

Go back to sleep. There isn't anyone, there never has been anyone.

Her voice answers him. He flinches, as if the sound isn't the one he was expecting.

'She's out there, Arden. Listen to her calling you. Let her in.'

He rolls over, lies straight on his back. He lifts his hand from his eyes and looks right through her over to the door.

'Elizabeth?' he says.

'No, not Elizabeth,' she says. 'You know her name, you've known for years. Say it now, the way she's saying yours. *Phil-ip, Phil-ip.* That's real enough for you, isn't it? Put her in between us, where she belongs.'

She takes the hand he's holding up. There's no resistance, the hand is limp as that of a sick person, a dead person. She bends his fingers with her own, makes the index finger form a circle with the thumb, as they did when he held up the cyanide pill.

'Where's the key, Philip?' she says. 'Show me where it is.'

He's mumbling so it's hard to hear.

I will disappear. It will be as though I had never been.

This is the moment at which she gives up on him, the moment that passes so quickly she's not even aware of it at the time. She drops his hand and scrambles off the bed. He's fallen into slow-motion, and if she's not quick she'll miss the moment that must follow, the moment when past and future and present all come together, when the doors all knock each other down like dominoes. The whine outside is getting fainter, giving up. She finds the light-switch, floods the room with light, stumbles to her bookshelves. Alphabetically ordered, as they always are.

W for Wells, but it's not there. She can't find it.

That's when she starts to scream. She screams with a woman's scream, shrill and hard enough to wake him fully, bring him gasping to the surface, flinging off the covers and falling from the bed onto his knees. She starts to drag the books out wholesale from the shelves, letting them fall like headland rocks, bouncing their weight down the hillside, onto the floor. She's looking for the dark blue cover that she knows so well, listening for the creak and split of the spine, the crack of fallen rulers, desk-lids.

She looks up and something in her shutdown brain says *Think.*

And there it is, top shelf where she can barely reach it, under A for Arden. She hears him roar at her like the tide but she jumps up and fetches it off the shelf, it and half a dozen others thumping to the floor, the white wings of their pages spread like grounded seagulls. And the key, jingling as it strikes the leather bindings, a light female tinkling like Pauline's charms; easy for her to snatch up, in the end, since Phil's so drunk and slow, fitted and turned in its lock before his feet have hit the floor.

She grabs the door. And she remembers, this is the one that opens towards her, and she pulls. The orange of the landing light fills up the dim bedroom. She steps across the threshold and the stairwell hollows dark above her, the stairs plunge downward like a waterfall. Phil pushes past her, and hand over hand stumbles down the stairs.

And there's no one there.

Wrong key, she thinks, *Wrong key.* And the thought rolls in her head like a stone, like a gravestone set rolling into the sea.

Then she looks down at the floor, and sees the spots of blood on the landing where she stood.

I sit on your stairs all night. All night, shouting myself hoarse and no one hearing me, no one coming. Just my voice vanishing up the stairwell and leaching out of a crack between the tiles, out into the dark blue sky, no tears in my eyes but something that I can't look at running down my legs, drizzling like raspberry sauce in faint weak streams down the stair-carpet. I shout out Philip's name and nothing else, I can't get past it, I can't let any other words out while it's there, like the old black egg bleached white,

156

like his hair, straw-dry from the peroxide. Down there in my stomach the voice is strong but with his name it evaporates, dissipates like a cloud.

I can't think why you don't answer me, why you don't come to the door. I know you're there, sleeping, living with him, the porter told me, but he didn't say your name and I won't ask. If I'd known it I would have had to call your name instead of his. I don't know if you understand that.

But eventually I quit, I give it up. I sit there and nothing happens. The quiet drops on me like a sodden blanket, lies on my head like fog, like the wrong kind of sleep. While I'm still able I get up, holding on to the banister, and walk myself carefully down the stairs, lots of stairs, hard despite the carpet on them, hard as stones rolled from the headland. My raspberry trail goes down with me, across the landing, down into the silent hall with the reception desk that smells of Pledge and the white unused blotter and the porter sitting in the back room with his feet up on the table and a rerun of Dynasty on the portable.

As I pass the desk I look over. The porter doesn't move.

Outside it's sunrise. Red sunrise, with the red round sun rising exactly in the centre of the bay, beaming a spotlight down across the flat sea and the low-tide empty beach with the little waves flapping softly against the sand. The sun casts the shadow of the obelisk on the promenade straight down the street, a shadow that seems like either a long dark column or a trench between the Esplanade and the other side of the road.

I don't remember which it feels to my feet. I just remember crossing it.

The King's Head has its lights on. The lights from an all-nighter, a lock-in. Except the front door isn't locked. The latch sticks out from the jamb like a silver tooth, but the door hasn't been shut properly, it gives when I push it. I look up and there's the landlord's name above the entrance. For a moment it stops me in my tracks, there's no way I can go back across that threshold. And then I hear something. Something sweet, like a mother's voice crooning a lullaby, supposing I could remember my mother singing to me.

It's Alex, of course. Alex, his neck swooping upward like a swan's, singing Misty.

The lock-in is well under way - it must be about four o'clock - but Alex has only just started his set. I hold my hand up but he's at the very top of his scale, he doesn't notice me, he doesn't see me through the smoke. The smoke inside the bar is like water, there's a knack to breathing it, there's a cool wet tang to it that blurs the people, fogs them as if they're underwater. I duck under someone's arm and head for the only vacant stool I can see, in front of a table shiny with beer-slops, and a woman's head and shoulders slumped across it. I tuck myself onto the stool and look at her. She has her cheek in beer-bubbles, bubbles that leave little white circles on her skin, like salt-marks. Her hands are ridged and crumpled with the sea-water, her fingernails short and flaky with the polish peeling off them. She's been running, the salt-marks prove it, running as far as she could and fished out of the sea before the water got her. And brought back. Brought here.

Then I understand something about the King's Head, or rather I understand the people in it, the people who are all sea-soaked, people who didn't quite make it to drowning, washed up in this bar. Washed up, other people say, and now it's true, it has a meaning. One day I will be like this woman. I know it, I look at her the way you look at an old snapshot. She feels familiar, a mixture of the past and future. And there are just the two of us together at the table, no Alex, most of all no Phil. I'm scared and not scared, calm in a way, because I feel like I can hear him at last.

There's one thing I know, with absolute certainty. I know that he'll come after me. If I want to escape - and there's no one here to stop me, least of all Alex - I don't have long to decide. Only if I make a run for it there's only one place to go, out onto the promenade and along the pier, gasping along the planks to the pier head bar, past the drinkers sitting outside at the picnic tables to the fishermen's platform at the end, with their lines trailing into the water, to the edge, with nothing left but falling or jumping, no comfort but Auntie Aileen's story about a God in Heaven who might put his arms out at the last minute and save me.

But I don't run straight away, I think about it. I see myself in my flowery nightie and shawl and flip-flops, with my toes clawed under trying to keep the flip-flops on, pushing my way through the crowd at the Amusement Arcade, with the noise from the slot machines flashing a turned-up pink and yellow that hurts my eyes. At the promenade end the path along the pier is narrow, there's always a squeeze of bodies and pushchairs and wheelchairs to slow you down. Then the boardwalk passes the Arcade and broadens out again, and the planks are stretched between lines of Victorian cast-iron railings that fence off the dark sea at the edges. And the sea breeze blows straight through the railings. But by this time I've lost the knack of running, my legs are like dream legs with no bones in them.

And I see myself limping past the roundabout and the children's slide, past the closed-down booths that offer to draw your baby or your pet, that sell flags and shell boxes and plaques with your name printed on them, past the locked toilets and the nailed-down tables outside the Pier Head Bar to the fishermen's platform. Land's End, they call *it, and I've never been on it before. At the very end of the pier there's a locked iron gate and a flight of metal steps leading down to a concrete slab where the fishermen stand. I see myself opening the iron gate and limping down the steep iron mesh steps, my nightie ballooning in the wind; and beneath me through the mesh I see thick soupy waves breaking on the legs of the pier. Out to sea it's dark with a few twinkly lights but most of all it's cold. My voice is frozen and I can't jump without my voice, and I can't fall because I'm afraid of falling. I try to sing, but it's only Misty I can hear, my own voice fainter and fainter in my head, losing me even in the middle of the bar.*

But I've been thinking for too long and he's coming for me. Over the heads of the customers I see the pub door open and close again. Just the top of the door, there are too many people in the bar to see who's coming through, but it's a hard push, the door springs back juddering after it. I knock my drink and the stool over, make a rush for the glass door at the back of the pub.

On the other side, the stairs leap upward in front of me. I grab the banister and haul myself upward but it's like the dream, I can't move properly, and until I get to the top I can't work out why. Then I look down and I realize the stairs are covered in wallpaper, great torn chunks of it sticking up like icebergs in the sea, flaps of it still clinging to the walls. And some trodden into scraps that stick to my feet. There's a trail of them along the dingy landing to my room at the furthest end.

The glass door opens again but it's hard for Phil to push it with the piles of paper on the floor. So I keep moving, backward this time, past the doors leading off the landing to the other bedrooms, 1, 2, 3, and finally 4, my room, the one you see right now and it's not changed so much, back then there's just woodchip on the walls and a beige standard lamp and a headless bed pushed back into the corner with an old red bedspread on it. And that's where I tumble down, leaning back as far as I can, and he keeps coming, he isn't going to stop.

His eyes are black. Somebody's opened them up, and it isn't me. Or it is me, it will be me. If I didn't have something to say, something shooting up my throat like a fountain, it feels as though I might die from the fear.

So I scream at him. Because there's only one fall left for me, and it isn't in this room.

'You've killed her,' I scream. 'Our little girl. Our Quetzal.'

I point down to the floor. There's blood on the carpet, a metaphor that isn't a metaphor any more but means just what it says. He looks, he doesn't stop himself in time, he doesn't close his eyes in time.

I don't see the hand before it hits me. There's just an x-ray left of it, no flesh, no nerves to feel anything. The hand passes through my cheek with the slow cold pain of a dentist's jab and then he's gone.

And I never speak of it again. I lock the door, my door, and after a long while, I don't know how long, I go out with Alex and together we find a grave for her, one where the lady looks the way I know Quetzal would have looked if she'd grown up and out into the world. And somehow, once we've found the grave, Philip comes back. Every Tuesday I watch the door and in he comes. But week by week, year by year, I can feel the chill spreading through his hands, like somebody dipped him in the sea. Growing colder, colder all the time.

It was pale blood, pink on the carpet, pink for a girl, she thinks. She remembers sitting on the bed and looking

161

through the open doorway at the blood, for a long time, she doesn't recall how long. And when he finally comes back up the stairs it's so slowly, and he sits on the end of the bed in his blue satin dressing gown, his hands clasped around one knee. His hair is still mussed up from sleeping, flattened to a corona of white roots and platinum ends springing from the centre of a round pink space of scalp. It's some time since he's coloured it, the native white is breaking through all over him. His memory is whiting out with the hair, the lines are giving up on him. She's right at his back, but he can't turn round and face her. But she's staying right where she is because as long as she keeps behind him he can't see her, he has to see the other woman.

Eventually he says

'Do you have a mirror?'

The triptych on the dressing-table won't do for him, least of all right now. She gets a compact from her bag and hands it over his left shoulder. He opens it and puts it up close to his face. He's looking for lines around his eyes, on his forehead underneath his fringe.

She pushes herself off the bed and walks slowly round until she's side-on to him.

He brings the mirror even closer, studying the regrowth underneath his fringe.

'I'll tell you something,' he says. 'I was dark once, kinda dusky chestnut, reddish tinge. She has a photo of me, agent's publicity still, before the bleach. No question, Arden had to have the bleach. I never did figure out why the stuff was blue.'

She touches her head. The scalp feels sore, as though he passed a feeling to her, the soreness passed through into her mind. *She.* He's said it, made it true.

'I would have liked an explanation,' she says.

'No explanation,' he says. 'Two lives, two sides of the road.'

'And what's in the middle?' she asks.

But she knows what's in the middle, she can see it from the window. What's at the end of everything, an obelisk pointing skyward like Elizabeth Horthy's plane, anchored to the earth by granite steps and circles of red flowers. Death and transfiguration. Arden gets his tabloid and his quiet place, but Wells doesn't say what happened to Elizabeth when her flying machine has taken her as far as it's going to, just talks about her stepping out onto the clouds. The heroic gesture, disappearance, death without the body. Jean doesn't even come in for that. She's frozen to the bed, trapped in her wig and greasepaint.

Like Phil, she thinks, *like Phil and not like me. I've got the casting wrong, it's all reversing on me again*. She looks out of the window and there are people crossing the road on the zebra just below the obelisk. Black, white, black, white. Opposites in bands, a sign of safety.

'Going back over there?' she asks.

He puts the compact down on the dressing table and starts to get dressed.

'Feel free to destroy all portraits,' he says.

She looks up at her bookshelves.

'I don't have any pictures to remember you by,' she says. 'Just words.'

He shrugs and takes a hairbrush from the dressing table, tries to force the white hair back across his emerging scalp.

'You must have had a real name once,' she says. 'I wonder what it is.'

He doesn't answer. Maybe he doesn't know. She watches him pulling on black jeans, sweatshirt, leather jacket, clothes no longer costuming but covering. His face is

163

turned away, he's saving up what's left of it for his final scene, keeping back the few lines he can still remember.

Does she know where he's going? She's not sure, but she knows what he's going to do. The only change she could make - to walk out there, not following him, but to cross the road to the King's Head that night - it's beyond her, without a guardian angel, someone to steady her through the dark, someone she's not yet able to admit might exist.

But that night she looks for her key, the one that says 21, and finds it gone. There's no frantic search this time, no further need for it any more, no reason to lock the door. She phones downstairs for the time of an early morning train, gets down a suitcase, and packs it. The books she leaves exactly where they fell, all except for *The Shape of Things to Come*. She picks it up, tears the flyleaf from the binding, lights her final cigarette and burns the inky paper. She's back exactly where she was before she fell into the hands of men; back except for her sham name, which she keeps by her as a warning. She closes the book, and replaces it on the bookshelf under W.

Then she lies down on the bed, alone, to sleep.

20

I wake up strangely, abruptly, as if someone was calling me
to wake up, someone I can hear but not see. My hands
sizzle with pins and needles, and there's a singing in my
ears, a giddiness. Perhaps I'm coming round from an
anesthetic I don't remember having, but when I sit up and
look around me I'm quite alone. The room is stuffy with the
window closed, so I get up to open it, wrapping myself in
the white dressing gown I find at the end of the bed.
Outside the day is half over and it's raining. The sea is grey
and white and stormy, and the onshore breeze wafts into
the room, blowing the curtains, making the wind-chimes
ring.

I go back and sit on the bed. My head is thick with
dreams, but the dream with the blonde woman in it won't
fade out. I can still hear her, knocking on my door like she
thought she was me, pushing her way through the blue
paint and the green paint and forcing her way into my
room, I can still hear the sucking and bursting of the paint
as the door tore open, I can smell the musk of her perfume.
But most of all I still hear her talking, her radio
announcer's voice so clear round the edges, as if she was
reading the news, and it was bad, all of it, it was the world
breaking in and taking away everything I knew, until in the
end I didn't know what was left. For a moment when I
woke I had an idea she was still sitting in the child's chair
but when I opened my eyes the chair was empty and I went
to the top of the stairs and called down them. I waited,
called again, but no one answered.

Then I knew she was gone.

On the bedside table she's left an old newspaper cutting, dated twenty years ago, about the body found on the beach. *Suicide*, it says; it's the last word of his life, there is no other. I slip the cutting into the drawer of the cabinet and leave it there. *I came to tell you he isn't coming back,* she said, and when I heard her say that I noticed the way she seemed to be listening to herself, as if she'd come all this way just to say it in this room. I don't know how I slept after that but I did, as though the years of waiting had worn me through, and when I woke up it was as if the room itself had vanished with him, and it was time for me to go too. Where I could go, I don't know: perhaps back across the bay to the small town where I was born, where there's sea, but no seaside, no hotels. Not a place for holidays, not for a long time now. Only I can't imagine what it will be like, living in a town with no hotels. I haven't been to the other side of the bay since we left, and I won't know a soul. My loneliness throbs in my head with the throb of toothache. A wisdom tooth, I think, deep, deep rooted in the head.

I don't want to go alone.

I look back at the empty chair. She's gone, and with her gone the seat has the shape of Alex in it again, Alex who I feel I haven't seen for so, so long, Alex who should be here right now.

I walk across the landing to run my bath, come back and lay out my clothes. I know you still love your clothes, Pauline said yesterday, so I didn't mind when she bought me a present, a long linen dress the colour of seaweed, not kelp-brown but the bright green of the weed that grows in long soft tresses on the rocks in summer, that only shows at low tide. The dress is new, it has the smell of newness, the creases from folds of fresh tissue paper, from the cardboard box. I felt like hugging Pauline when I opened it, even shaking hands with Ralph, but I restrained myself. I've had so many parents.

While I'm in the bath I sing. Angels is my favourite, and Perfect Day, but I can't keep them up for long. I tell myself that it's the singing that counts, the feeling of not being chased away. Though I haven't forgotten the jukebox songs, not a scrap of tune, not a word. By afternoon they've re-established themselves, creeping back into my head. The long-term memories, the ones that are the last to go.

I remember every word.

When I'm dressed I go and look at myself in the mirror. There's still a wave in my hair from the perm six months ago, still about a foot of blondeness from my forehead to my shoulders, though an inch or so of root is showing dark. I was never what you'd call a blonde, not with the hint of salmon pink in my colour, but now the dark is striped with grey a paler tint is best. In the bathroom cabinet the two bottles of hair dye, his and mine, are still there on the top shelf, but I won't be tempted to use the blue one, not even now. I saw him using it too often, saw how it stripped the colour out with acid, drained the dark away down the plughole, left him dazzling with his blind whiteness. My face couldn't take that, my eyes would give me away, taking up more of my face than they used to do, my lids are swimmer's eyelids, red and tender and a little swollen.

I turn to show the profile of my body to the mirror. My stomach pushes through the green like a stubborn stone, the backs of my arms sprout narrow flesh-wings. I hug myself and spread the fingers out to hide the wings. The dress is sleeveless, and my flesh is cold. I want something to cover it, not something new but something I know, something familiar, an old warm skin, the fur coat Alex used to wear, his old suede jacket.

Sweet Alex.

The rain has stopped, as it often does about this time. The promenade is gleaming in the low rays of five o'clock sunshine, and people are appearing from the hotels to have their pre-dinner constitutionals, marching smartly down the steps with the gait of old soldiers at the Albert Hall. I find my make-up bag and start to paint my face: peach cream base, rose madder cheeks, green shadow to counteract the red eyelids, black eyeliner to sharpen. I'm going out, to Karaoke Night at the Pier Head Bar, to find Alex. Out of habit I look across the road, but the curtains are drawn across the windows, the way they are when someone dies. Except I know now that those who died went long ago. What I'm seeing is an after-image, the light of understanding finally reaching me across the galaxies.

And what I don't see yet, he'll show to me. He'll make everything clear, as clear as water.

I step out into the sunshine. I'd forgotten how it blinds you, forgotten how the wind whips up your hair and clothes. I wish I had my shawl to wrap around me, but I've left it folded neatly in my room, together with a pile of clothes to go to Sapphire. I dash across the road to the prom and the wrought-iron gates leading onto the pier. At sunset they'll be locked, and then the only people able to get out will be the night fishermen with their pass-keys and their rods, their catch swinging silver beside them.

I slip myself into the crowd. At the promenade end the pier boardwalk is narrowed by the Amusement Arcade on the left, slot machines ringing and flashing pink and yellow. The boards are dark and slippery with water beside the Fire Brigade booth, where children fire off water pistols at imaginary blazes. The dark iron legs of the pier stilt out across the stones and on towards the sea. Beyond the arcade the boardwalk broadens out again and the squeeze of bodies resolves itself into pushchairs, wheelchairs, toddlers, parents.

The peaked roofs of the souvenir kiosks shine, still wet, painted for the season with fresh pale blue paint. They were closed down in the rain but now the sellers are opening up again, encouraged by the prospect of a warm late summer's evening. As I pass the kiosk where I bought my wind-chimes the woman with the black curls is taking down the shutters. The breeze blows into the open door and there's a tinkling, a movement of hanging gems of glass and mirror-squares that flash their semaphore from the interior. *The Crystal Cave,* the booth is called. A good sign, a good omen, if I still believed in such things.

Almost at the end of the pier is the long low Victorian building with its ornamental dome that was once a theatre and now houses more slot-machines. Where the building spreads its width across the pier the boardwalk forks to circumvent it, so that from the air the pier would look like a capital Y, with the old theatre in the centre of the letter and the cafe and Pier Head Bar in the right and left points of the fork.

Once past the arcade entrance I go left, contouring around the long curve of the theatre wall towards the outside picnic tables where most of the drinkers are gathered, hunched backs to the sea breeze, waiting for the karaoke to start. The bar is almost empty, the lights on the karaoke machine lit up but still, waiting to flash in time to the music. On the small raised platform that passes for a stage a man with a ponytail is wrestling with plugs and flexes.

I go and buy myself a drink. I can't see Alex anywhere.

Time passes and the sun dips lower. The music starts and the lights flash on and off sporadically. A few of the outside drinkers drift into the bar, but not many. I finish my drink, and get up to buy another. The song playing is the one Alex always dedicated to me, *Love Grows Where my Rosemary Goes.* The man with the ponytail looks up as I get to my feet, holds out the microphone to me.

'Why don't you get us started, love,' he says. 'You were here first, after all.'

I stand still. He switches on a small spotlight, turns it on me and one or two people clap slowly, ironically. I take the microphone and hold it against my chest where the green dress forms a V. The black sponge is soft, warm from the electric current, sizzling static against my skin. Instead of my voice it picks up the thump of my heart, sends it round the room. The clappers start to laugh, and take up the beat with their hands. I begin to speak, not to the man but to the room at large, except that nobody can hear me. I move the microphone closer to my mouth.

'I'm looking for someone,' my voice says through the speakers. 'Sandy Laine. He used to sing here, years ago.'

Then they hear me, they put down their drinks and look up, and I hear the feedback in my voice, as if I asked the question twice, but nobody answers. The neon bulbs flash pink and yellow in time with my words, but it's the real light I'm facing, the sun that's finally found an opening beneath the half-closed window-blinds and flooded the wooden floor. I hand back the microphone and look over to the doorway. It's getting brighter outside by the minute.

The thumping of my heart has made its way into my ears. It's a strange sound, a deep beat with a lesser one following it, a ghost beat, the beating of two hearts. As I move outside into the sunlight flood the sound doesn't disappear but grows louder, I feel it vibrating through the boards at my feet. Only the second sound vibrates, though, only the ghost beat. The first beat is sound alone.

I turn and look to my left, past the corner of the bar to the blue safety rail bordering the end of the pier. The sound in my feet grows louder. A couple of yards short of the rail a little girl is playing with a red ball, throwing it against the end wall of the old theatre, letting it bounce once on the boardwalk, then catching it and beginning again. She has on a pink dress and ankle-socks, and a cardigan with pom-poms swinging from the neck, pom-poms that bounce when she throws. The child is alone, no parent in sight, none of the people leaning over the rail to watch the fishermen taking any notice of her.

I take a couple of steps forward and then stop, my feet touching one another as if standing to attention. As the child feels my gaze she looks away from her ball-game and at me, and the ball leaves her hand skewed, striking the theatre wall low down and shooting off across the boards, in small skipping bounces, rolling through the rail and disappearing off the end of the pier.

I wait for the sound of the splash, but it doesn't come. The child runs up to the rail and grips the top bar with outstretched hands, and begins to cry.

I go up to her and cover her hands with my own. There is no resistance, just the warm stickiness of her fingers, the heat of her grip on the rail. She's not cold after all, not dead, not white, not hard as the truth. She turns her wet face to me and her colours are just as I imagined them, the mousy hair and the hazel eyes and the sallow August-tinted skin with the burnt umber tip of nose. She lifts my right hand up with her own and points downward to the sea. Below us the waves slap on the green barnacled lower platform and the concrete pillars that hold the grey slab of Land's End, as if in suspension, above it. I see helpless red and yellow jellyfish swaying in the current, I see the red ball bobbing with the flotsam underneath the pier.

171

I take a breath. The air has a fishy smell, though there's no sign of any catch on the trailing lines, barely visible, stretched into the water.

She turns, stretching my arm out, pointing back down the pier.

That's where we bought it, she says. *It was the last one left.*

Her nose drips soft pendants. She needs her hands back.

'It's all right,' I say. 'I'll get it for you.'

I let her hands go. I feel her arms go round me, feel the lifebelt of warmth pressing deep into my stomach, see the smile.

I love you, she says.

She steps back, and I'm alone. I put my hand on the catch of the iron gate leading down to Land's End. I peer over the gate, my green skirt billowing around me in the wind. On the concrete platform below me the fishermen stand still as a postcard, their backs to me, rods fringing the platform. The red ball is still there, coming and going against the uprights of the pier, at first reachable from solid stone and then at sea again. I'll have to climb down the steps and get into the water, tread water, keep myself afloat. My hands and feet are cold on the rail but round my middle I've got the warmth of my lifebelt.

Behind me I can feel my little girl still there, right in the centre of the boardwalk, watching everything I do. If I leave the ball and climb back down she'll disappear.

I shut my eyes as the sea heaves another wave onto the platform. The wave is green and swells with something, the size and shape of a body, glazed with water but visible just below the surface. The moon swings and the wave recedes, stranding its ballast on the platform, a growl of barnacles following its retreat. I grip the gate and start to turn my face away. I know I'm seeing how Philip died, not only how the

172

sea caught him but how he fell, dropping endlessly through my memory, how he was washed up like a dogfish on the beach; and No, I think, I can't look now, and then the words are breaking from my mouth the way they did in the church all those years ago; *Help me*, I'm saying, *Save me*, and then there's another voice in my head, singing *Misty*, just one last encore at the Pier Head Bar. Suddenly I can see Alex in his wedding hat, his wings blowing out behind him, holding out his hand to me; and I touch his bones, his fingers, and he's cold as Christmas. Soft though, sad though, not hard.

Angels are high up, I hear myself say to him. *High up, and you're low down, the way you've always been.*

Saved is all that matters, he says to me. *Washed up is all it means, wet and straggling like the rest of us have been for years.*

But they've all gone now, I say. *Everyone disappears. Even you.*

Megan, darling, he says, *Didn't your friend tell you? Everyone dies, or not quite everyone.*

I look up and shake my head and he points to the water and says, *Follow him, or don't follow him. Be lost, or found. Can't have it both ways.*

Save me then, I say, and my body tips outward, dips toward the waves.

And just before I let go of the rail I see the red ball bobbing on the swell beneath me and I remember something she said and I think

The book was not the last of the signs

And I take a breath.

'Let it go, little one,' I say. 'Let it go.'

I release her hands. I feel her arms go from around me, her warmth folded deep into my stomach, softening it, warming the last month's blood held there in suspension, waiting for the moment of release.

She steps backward, folding softly into the crowd, waving a sunburnt hand.

Bye, bye, Mummy, she says.

The water's flooding my eyes but through it I see the red ball on the green water, bobbing out from underneath the pier, pulled far out into the waves until it's a red pool, then a spot, and finally nothing. I wipe my eyes and start to move, dragging myself slowly back along the boardwalk, until I realize how deserted it is, that I'm the last person on the pier and it's nearly sunset, time for the gates to be locked. My loneliness knocks against my stomach like a wave striking the pier; and I stumble, clutch my body, don't quite fall.

Ahead of me, at the gates, somebody calls.

'Come on, love. Time to go home.'

As I break into a run I see the man with the keys, holding them up, a quick flash of red in the sunset; and beyond the gates the obelisk, flowers all around it, red circles for those who've disappeared, who aren't ever coming back. I pick up my green skirts and run through the closing gates and keep running until I see her, waiting for me, hair platinum in the sunshine, a wreath of poppies for the grave held in her arms.

White, red, white.

Roberta Dewa began writing in her twenties and her first published novel was a defence of bad King John.

While studying for various degrees she wrote and published poetry and short fiction, including a poetry sequence on the explorer Shackleton, and her first short story collection, *Holding Stones* (Pewter Rose Press, 2009).

Recently she has returned to full-length works. In 2013 she published her memoir, *The Memory of Bridges,* a return to the village of her childhood, and a search for her mother's history.
The Esplanade is her first contemporary novel.

When not writing, Roberta teaches at the University of Nottingham.

www.robertadewa.co.uk

Acknowledgements

First, I'd like to thank those who were there at the beginning of this journey: from my time at NTU, Diana Peasey, Vicky Joynson, and Joy Armstrong; and Graham Joyce, for some characteristically tough love.

I also want to send heartfelt thanks to Megan Taylor for her insights and clear-sightedness when working with me on the revising of this novel, for her unfailing support and encouragement, and for her invariably wise suggestions about the text.

Finally, and in a very similar vein, I want to thank Ian Collinson for his general wisdom and sensitivity in working through the later stages of the novel with me, for his support and patience, and for helping me to stay the course.

Cover painting by Kit Wade
www.kit-wade.co.uk

Author photo by FLUK Studios